Praise for FEM

"*FEM* is a protes[...] th the fervor of a true poet, a [...] nen in a still male-dominated [...] ...dicalism, this novel's readers will discover an impressive quality of mind and artistic refinement that attract our empathy."

—Mircea Cărtărescu,
author of *Solenoid, Nostalgia,* and *Blinding*

"Poet Cârneci's rich English-language debut records a woman's dreamlike ecstatic experiences and revelations...Full of strong imagery, this heavily symbolic work is a notable entry in international feminist literature." —*Publishers Weekly*

"Magda Cârneci is not only a distinguished poet, translator, and art critic but a first-rate novelist, who uses her storytelling gifts in *FEM* to open new worlds for the silent auditor of her strange visions. The narrator describes herself as "a tamer Scheherazade," but she is fierce in her quest to charm, instruct, and awaken readers to the particular challenges of a woman picking her way through the maze of modern life. These tales, spun from seemingly inconsequential moments into existential reflections on the nature of everything under the sun, will haunt your days and nights."

—Christopher Merrill, author of *Self-Portrait with Dogwood*

"Hard to sum up in just a few words, *FEM* is a psychedelic novel about the essences of femininity. A poetic prose that left me with the impression that it would fit wonderfully into a new wave of aesthetic oneiricism. A novel for the cognoscenti, *FEM* is scandalous and provocative in equal measure." —Marius Mihet

FEM

Magda Cârneci

Translated from the Romanian
by Sean Cotter

DEEP VELLUM PUBLISHING

DALLAS, TEXAS

Deep Vellum Publishing
3000 Commerce St., Dallas, Texas 75226
deepvellum.org · @deepvellum

Deep Vellum is a 501c3 nonprofit literary arts organization
founded in 2013 with the mission to bring
the world into conversation through literature.

Support for this publication has been provided in part by grants from the
National Endowment for the Arts and the Romanian Cultural Institute's
Translation and Publication Support program.

ISBNs: 978-1-64605-041-3 (paperback) | 978-1-64605-042-0 (ebook)

LIBRARY OF CONGRESS CATALOGING IN PUBLICATION DATA

Names: Cârneci, Magda, author. | Cotter, Sean, 1971- translator.
Title: Fem / Magda Cârneci ; translated from the Romanian by Sean Cotter.
Other titles: Fem. English
Description: Dallas, Texas : Deep Vellum Publishing, [2020] | "Originally
  published in 2011 by Editura Polirom in Bucharest, Romania"
Identifiers: LCCN 2020044994 (print) | LCCN 2020044995 (ebook) | ISBN
  9781646050413 (trade paperback) | ISBN 9781646050420 (ebook)
Classification: LCC PC840.13.A77 F4613 2020 (print) | LCC PC840.13.A77
  (ebook) | DDC 859/.335--dc23
LC record available at https://lccn.loc.gov/2020044994
LC ebook record available at https://lccn.loc.gov/2020044995

Cover Design by Victoria Peña

Interior Layout and Typesetting by KGT

PRINTED IN THE UNITED STATES OF AMERICA

This is a work of fiction. Names, characters, places, and incidents either are
the product of the author's imagination or are used fictitiously, and any re-
semblance to actual persons, living or dead, businesses, companies, events, or
locales is entirely coincidental.

FOR YOUTH, UNDYING

The work of a visionary is to see; and if he narrows himself in activities that eclipse God and prevent him from seeing, he betrays not only his better being, but also those like him, who have the right to vision.
—Aldous Huxley, *The Doors of Perception*

The imaginary is what tends to become real.
—André Breton

Writing is a religious act outside of all religions.
—Georges Perros

FEM

BEGINNING THE JOURNEY

Darling, don't be scared. I have a secret: I am a kind of Schehe-
razade. A little, everyday Scheherazade in an ordinary neigh-
borhood, in a provincial city; your personal Scheherazade, even
if you won't cut my head off in the morning, when I fail to
keep you awake all night with extraordinary stories. You can
find those on television; I know all too well how you spend your
evenings: you ingest vast amounts of news programs and cop
shows and soap operas and porn and documentaries and every-
thing else . . . I won't become another screen and antenna for
you, I won't tell you about airplane crashes, highway accidents,
rapes, about the latest war to break out, which politician is the
most corrupt, the latest rock star to kill himself, the new crop
of starlets for this season, how many people died in the terror-
ist attack, and all the other bitter tidbits you use, one evening
after the next, to drug the neural pathways in your worn-out
brain. You consume too much audiovisual garbage, on top of
your problems at work and the vodka and beer and wine you
pour down your throat, stubbornly, aggressively, even spitefully,

11

sprawled across the couch for hours at a time, facing a screen that pours all the terrors and horrors of the world into you.

No, stay calm, I'm not here to preach, I will be a tamer Scheherazade, I'll tell you stories about me, about us, about the small but odd things we pass over without noticing, amazing but normal stories, mysterious scenes we usually forget, which our memory sets aside out of stubbornness or fear. I will tell you about me, and you about you, and even us about us, and if it doesn't seem important to you, if your life, if our life has no value, and its odd stories have even less, I will tell them nevertheless. In fact, you are a bit of a hypocrite; all anyone wants is to talk about themselves, to hear themselves talking about themselves, to be listened to, listened to for a long time, but not to listen. And, in fact, if one person truly listens to another, that person feels as though he's speaking to the entire world, as though all of humanity is listening. He feels fulfilled in his vocation, his destiny, if only one person will listen to him. But most people don't know how to listen, they are timid, they are afraid of themselves and others, and so they keep to the banalities of daily life, family troubles, jokes they've heard, scandals they've read about in the paper. A kind of comfortable numbness, a kind of stubborn forgetting, a void in their lives makes them focus on insignificant things. But something eats at them, bothers them; from time to time, a sort of longing, a strange absence troubles their amnesia and their sleep. Every person looks for someone to listen to them, all the way to the end, someone to whom they can open up their depths and who will inspire them to be what they could be, and what, in their essence, they are.

Darling, I don't want to overwhelm you, to pelt you with who knows what hypothesis and theory; I will be a simpler Scheherazade, I won't bombard you with stylistic experiments, with demonstrations of verbal virtuosity, with linguistic charades. I've done that before, but I've gotten better, I'm over that illness, that metabolic growth. Now I am looking for experiences and visions. I hunt special, radiant states, I search for concentrated, powerful images. In this life, states like these come seldom, and never the same way twice, states like these always take us by surprise, they insist on the presence of something pre-existent within us, or without, something that waits to be discovered. States like these seem to open hidden channels within our being, channels that are ordinarily obscure, hermetically sealed. Strange inner images, excessively intense, springing from an unknown source, from the depths of the unconscious or from the supersensorial abyss, that leave a pulsating, unerasable imprint on the circumvolutions of our overstuffed and over-stressed cerebral hemispheres hypnotized by the outside world. These floating visions seem to want to say something, to break open a valve of consciousness, to show the way toward levels of our being unknown to us, undeveloped, perhaps, or forgotten.

And all of these states, images, visions exist and await within you, darling, in the little television of vibrations buried in your flesh and being, they await your experience and reexperience, they are waiting to be discovered and contemplated, waiting for you to remember. To access something, something essential within you—as bored, as tired, as sound asleep as you are, something that will keep you awake the rest of your life. I will be a kind of Scheherazade.

PROLOGUE

They say that men and women are improvising actors, anxious dilettantes, pushed for an hour onto a brightly lit theater stage or studio set for a short public presentation in between the nothing that precedes and the nothing that follows the play, the nebulousness where they must act. Let us take, for example, a woman. She reaches the set only after she has passed through warehouses and basements full of slightly worn props, musical instruments fallen from use, and broken marionettes; then corridors, orchestra pits, wings, with piles of put-away props. Before climbing onstage, the woman has vagabonded through the store of period costumes, trying some on, then others, leaving them on the floor, sticking a child's shoe in her pocket or palming a piece of glass jewelry. She has wandered among plaster animals, country landscapes, or mountains made of cardboard and sticks. She has dawdled in a small Greek amphitheater, then in a Roman arena, she has climbed a small, pointed mountain full of hermit caves, round holes dug into the rock, she has hidden behind the altar of a baroque cathedral with walls of stained glass, she has fought the redskins in an American village, she has colonized a piece of the jungle, forgetting things here and there along the way: a key, an ID card, her sunglasses.

Only after she has lost countless hours among the wings, corridors, and overstuffed closets, among the control rooms packed with monitors, recording devices, and speakers playing all kinds of things—sports, political protests, classical concerts, jazz, rock—only after she has passed through makeup rooms with heaps of bras, belts, shawls, corsets, hats, suits of armor, and other bits of harness, does someone come to push her suddenly onto an immense, shimmering platform. Blinded by the strong spotlights, the woman sees the black space surrounding her, she hears a host of technicians and operators breathing, watching her coolly, professionally, and she is overtaken by a sudden nervousness and a strong fear. She knows her only option is to play the role they dressed her for—quickly in the wings with a costume on her body and a mask on her face, just before they pushed her in front of the spotlights. In that moment she forgets everything she saw before, and, trembling, she focuses on the present as much as she can, she tries to keep her hand on the reins, she keeps her mind on the other actors and the scenery, she takes everything seriously and acts. She plays. She plays a role she does not know, one that no one gave her to memorize ahead of time, one that she does not remember.

Under the blinding spotlights, in the moments of these seemingly endless short plays, the woman forgets her previous ramblings through the storerooms and scenery; it seems to her that everything comes down to this: a stage bathed in light, surrounded by darkness. It seems to her that nothing else exists, not before or after. Nothing. Only from time to time, when a fleeting image, something sporadic, uncannily clear and strange, disturbs her mind for a short second, does she confusedly remember the props and period costumes, the far-off rooms and wings, and the next moment she forgets them all again. The woman believes that everything comes down to this so powerfully illuminated stage, where she acts, she plays, tormented by the worry she won't find a quick reply to the other actors, who are also improvising; she is terrified she will play her part wrong, a part she intuits but does not know, tortured by fear of the darkness she sees around her. At times, a brusque quaking through her bones and muscles, or flashes of light through her eyeballs, or eddies within her cranium make her stutter loudly, or suddenly fall quiet; they almost prevent her from acting, as though she had touched an electrical outlet, a high voltage, a superior voltage. An outlet she encountered by mistake, electricity that propels her beyond her improvised and uncertain acting, laterally, toward a parallel world of strange and abnormal states.

Wouldn't she feel calmer if she could make the effort to remember, at least occasionally, briefly but intensely, her peregrinations through the wings, free movement past the scenery and the orchestra pits, before she was taken and sent for her interminable hour upon this blindingly lit stage? Wouldn't she feel more reconciled to her position if she strove to try to see, flicking her gaze, just for a short second, toward the wings from whence she came, or even better, toward the wings on the other side, in the direction of her exit?

To attempt to perceive the props stacked over there, the unknown scenes where she has yet to venture, the backdrops painted with lunar craters or the glittering gates of a glass-jeweled Jerusalem, or plaster and cardboard models of strange, unknown creatures with thousands of wings in the colors of the rainbow, cosmic vessels in the shapes of gods and stars, novel musical instruments, folding chairs and translucid ladders, all with such odd shapes, such ascendance . . .

The hidden movements in the play, the unknown or indifferent or hostile actors, the overly artificial, overpowered lights, the banal or complicated or absurd roles she has to improvise as she goes, nothing gives the woman enough time to concentrate, enough space to let her remember something from before or after, abnormal images, little electric earthquakes, flashes of a transfigured world in flight. She doesn't even have time to turn her head. She lives in the pain of a strange hypnosis, a kind of terror, beneath the harsh spotlights, before the darkness she sees around her. And I wonder, if she had just a moment to breathe, a moment's peace, if suddenly the spotlights, the scenery, the other actors all disappeared into the dark and the woman was left by herself, in a deep and restful calm, what more would she want, what would she remember to do? Would she find the courage to look into the pits piled with leftover epochs, to remember where she came from, and to run, to run away from the gilded prison of this stage? Would she want to turn her head suddenly toward the exit, to see the prompter holding the text, gesturing next to his lamp, while through the strange, fantastic props, the man who directs, no, the woman who directs the show, holding a round mirror, runs off?

MY BODY

I sat there, on the green bench in the city park, in the desolate and luminous morning, thinking about myself for the millionth time. Why wasn't it working, what was wrong with me, where did I go wrong? I stared without blinking, almost hypnotized, at the sycamore trunks stained white and brown, damp with dew. Why was I not satisfied with myself, what was not right? The bench was old and rickety, the green paint was peeling, and underneath you could see a lighter color, whitish-yellow, like an old leper.

Then I stared for a long time, hungrily, at my young body, my hands, arms, chest, I passed quickly over my abdomen, slowly over my legs. I studied my pointed white shoes, as though I were seeing them for the first time. At that moment, a brown ant was hurrying over the tip of the left shoe. What is happening, why aren't I right with myself, what have I forgotten, what don't I understand? Obsessively, the same thoughts passed through my mind, as my unsettled gaze rose over the transparent nylon socks wrapping my thin calves, then the gently curved thighs under the white dress I had on. I drew my eyes slowly, more and more curious, over my womb, domed somewhat, then I came to the bodice, I held my gaze on my breasts, as though I were surprised by their round crests, beneath the dress. For a second I imagined my small, flat sex, pressed between my thighs, indifferent, providing me no sensations. Then I embraced myself in a single gaze, head to toe, seated politely on a green and slightly damp bench. I tried to understand my body, to love it. It seemed so strange, this body which enclosed me as though in a hermetic box, this liveried and absurd body, as though it had grown by itself, without any effort on my part; I almost couldn't recognize it, it almost wasn't mine. A kind of surprised pity passed through me, mixed with disgust. Who had stuck me in this pinkish-white package, from which I could never extract myself? Who had put me, without the possibility of escape, in this uniform of flesh, bone, and hair, with limbs that ended in ridiculous protuberances, with hands and feet that ended in claws?

I looked around me at the park. Noisy packs of students skipping school passed down the path in front of me, then an older man with a cane and white straw hat, two old women hauling a voluminous sack, a nanny pushing a bright, white stroller. Young couples passed, kissing hungrily, almost biting each other, then some stumbling drunk soldiers, and a lone high school girl, small and clutching her elbows. I stared at each of them in turn; I saw another old woman, a lady in a hurry, another girl. Young women, like me, timid and trembling like reeds, mature women sure of themselves, like proud, multi-colored battle towers with feathered turrets, then aged women, resigned like sad, smoldering ruins. I stared at them, marveling at their existence, that women existed, like me, many women, so many women, it seemed so bizarre . . . this multitude of versions of me, these almost identical copies . . .

Their existence seemed more incredible to me than the existence of men. Them I accepted, so obvious, massive, self-important, self-evident. Weren't they the important ones, the true and the strong, as my father would say? But women, how could they exist? And for what? This something so incongruent, fragile, so mixed-up and hidden . . . I looked at them from the front, the side, the back, I marveled at how they moved freely through space, forced by no one, independent of me, the surprising, undulating forms of their bodies. At once beautiful and odious. Extravagant and base. Exhilarated yet pitiful. I looked at myself again, wrapped in a white dress, and I could not stop wondering at the fact that I existed, in this impossible form, one so contradictory, unacceptable, painful. And it made me ill, I felt an empty spot under my diaphragm, in my solar plexus, just as I did whenever I was in some physical danger, or facing some difficult and important decision. Something was not right with me, that much was clear; something was missing. But what, exactly?

On the green bench. In the park. Where did this evil come from? I repeated the question in my head, dizzy, holding myself with my arms as though I were suddenly cold. Why don't I like myself, what can't I accept, what am I missing? Where did I get the idea that I had made a mistake somewhere, that I had forgotten something important? Sometimes I understood myself without a sex, as though I woke up in the morning like a newborn with nothing between my legs, only to remember later that I have to put a costume on, not even mine, even though I keep it at my house. The costume is arcane and complicated, uncomfortable but luxurious, full of skirts, bows, zippers, embroidery; it is a costume I have to take care of constantly, to brush, clean, and repair. A borrowed costume, one I have to employ with a certain seriousness if I want to play my part, *my part*—who knows who chose this part for me, who gave me this burden, who trained me, who forced it into my reflexes and brain. And precisely the strange, glossy gazes of the men I encountered on the street each morning abruptly reminded me to play the part again, to identify myself with the uniform

I brought from home. Clearly, by now I don't even know if I could play another part; I've been in this bizarre costume, some even call it beautiful, from the start; I could have been born a dog or a cat, a sheep or a wild goat, a platypus or an orangutan, a crocodile or an elephant, I could have come into this world an earthworm or a bee, or a sparrow, or a snake—so what didn't I like about my young, supple body, what was wrong with me, what had I forgotten, what was my mistake?

I sat there for a long time on the rickety, green bench, watching people pass. There were men and women and children, women, women, many women. I was also a young woman, like the others, one of hundreds of women, one of thousands and millions of women in this hypnotic reality, and I could not grasp it. This curious division of one person into two. Like a gold coin broken awkwardly into two nonidentical halves. And yet identical. No, nonidentical. And yet the same. Something absurd, un-understandable, something unbearable. Like a black flash that burns through the neural filaments, like a blade that cuts, that cleaves the brain, splits what was unified and harmonious, whole, exultant, the luminous, perfect sphere. The park paths spread like a labyrinth around my green, rickety bench, the trees cast blue shadows over the freshly mown and watered lawn; then, glancing down, I noticed a kind of grand, multipetaled rose in the irregular cracks in the asphalt. I stared, more and more absorbed, at these almost perfectly circular cracks, full of dark dust and bits of grass, unraveling from a deep, unseen center, like a flower that shows and at the same time hides its obscure, tenebrous core. An ashen, asphalt rose, like a drop of gray lava, compressed and solidified, over whose convolutions my mind began to drift, undulating, expanding. Lifting my gaze, I saw a vaster, vaporous rose in the white clouds in the sky, their irregular edges tinged with gold and pink, slowly spreading, unraveling like a quiet floral explosion against the luminous azure expanse.

Then a woman passed my bench, she was tall, haughty, a strangely beautiful woman. Her beauty shocked me, for a moment I couldn't breathe. Her face showed an unbelievable harmony, unbearable to look at, impossible to withstand, so complete, such distinct nobility. As though in a trance, or by magnetic attraction, I rose from the bench and followed this proud woman, I followed her down the paths of the park. Her figure, her gait reminded me of something, something mysterious, something I knew long ago, but what? As I followed her at a distance, an intense and strange image suddenly erupted from inside me; in my mind, in a flash, I relived a fragment of an old dream: on the peak of a perfectly conical mountain, not far away, a tall and haughty woman, a goddess—draped in a purple cloak with gold embroidery, outlined by a narrow halo of light—waved to me, she beckoned me to climb toward her, she called me to her.

When the flash of this inner vision had passed, I saw the tall and haughty woman again, moving quickly away, her perfect figure disappeared beyond the wrought iron gate at the park's main entrance. I ran after her, I took the street I thought she had taken, but I could not find her. She was gone. I ran through the streets for a while, the idea of losing her seemed unbearable, I felt that inside her, in that woman, was a hidden key, a vital answer, something crucial for me, but what? Then I became tired, I stopped, I gave up. I turned slowly back toward the park. I looked around at people's faces, I thought I spied fragments of that magisterial beauty in the face of a teenager, in a child's gaze, but it was not the same, it was not her. I seemed ridiculous even to myself, I was like a lover who thought he saw his lost love everywhere, in every woman, even in men, in all the people he encountered, as though a precious hologram were broken into thousands of fragments and shards, and every shard held a bit of an image, an allusion, a glimpse of the whole face, of the face of his beloved.

In the end, exhausted, I turned back to my green park bench, I laid down and drifted off to sleep. I don't know how long I was asleep, in the cool air of the bright and sunny morning. When I opened my eyes again, a few meters before me on the path, I saw another woman, completely different from the one I had just lost. She was a squat housewife, with a round, hard face, a square body, and modest dress, holding hands with two children, two girls, in yellow and white overalls. And I remembered an old, yellowed photograph of a young woman holding two children wearing overalls, a photo I had hidden in an old diary and forgotten. And in that moment, something broke inside me, and an avalanche of images flowed from within. Something like a movie flooded me inside.

The First Awakening

Oh, Mother, bittersweet, ubiquitous Mother, from your uterine heaven, you look at me with your black, cyclopean eye. You follow my slips, my falls, ever lower and lower, across roofs, asphalt streets, couches, tables, the parquet floor of my room, I feel you always near. Hypnotic gorgon, paralyzing Medusa, you watch me steadily and coldly, from the east to the west, from behind my things strewn about the room, you watch me with a circular, pink face.

Oh, mother, bittersweet honey, enormous female, all-encompassing, in whom I am lost, drowned, like a poppyseed in a cloud of cotton candy. Suffocating, sticky candy cloud, where I want to dissolve, happily, to lie buried under layers of soft fog and ancient fat. I want to wrench myself, to extract myself, to run away through a swamp that tenaciously pulls me down, a formless dough that immobilizes my legs.

I was in a summer garden, one full of flowers of all

colors and scents. I peered at the root of each long, sharp blade of grass, among the giant black beetles and hurrying brown ants, at the large, polyhedral threads of dust bounding over the enormous, shining insects. I saw thin rivulets of milk and honey, like glittering chords, flowing through the air. I communicated through melodic vibrations with a range of chirping birds.

Then you came, monstrous pachyderm, you were a shadow of unraveling darkness that reached the stars, your passing filled the garden with clangs and bangs. You stopped in front of my wavelength. I had just been speaking with a sunray. You wanted to fill your basket, to satiate your swollen stomach. You smiled at me with fancy and sweetness, you revealed your heavy, pink-purple breasts. You gathered me in, you swallowed me, you sowed me within you. Within your soft trove of flesh, within the sweet-tasting hot earth from the bottom of a small sarcophagus. The sarcophagus was still empty, its walls were painted with vines heavy with minuscule blue grapes, and above them, swarms of bees. And in the distance, there was a great darkness over a tall and red gate of flesh.

Ma.

Ma. Ma.

Mba. Pa. Pa.

Mpa. Rockabye, child.

Ma. Sleep, darling. Pa. Quiet, be quiet with Mamma. Mba.

You want your Papa? Pa. You want to go peepee? Pa. Mba, ba.

Come to Mamma. Ma. Ma. Come to Papa. Pa. Pa.

Come, sweetie. Ma—ma. Bravo, that's it. Pa—pa.

How big you are. Mamma. Papa. Daddy. Don't wet yourself.

Mm. Yes, yes . . .

The child drinks milk. She drinks warm milk from a white porcelain cup. The child turns the white, liquid milk into white, muscular milk, chubby milk. She flings it joyfully about. She drinks in big gulps, thirsty. The child turns the white, liquid god into the sweet, pampered god. Everything is white, warm, and sweet. God is warm, white, and good-tasting. Sweet. Sweet. But then someone comes and snatches the cup from the child. And the milk. And the white image. God goes dark.

I am almost four years old. In yellow, flowered overalls, I sit politely on a chair. With my back against a playpen made of wood, painted white, with shiny metal bars. In front of me is an orchard. Large, very large trees climb to the sky. Fruit trees. Pears and apples. There are red apples on the ground. The apples are pretty. There are pears on the ground. The pears are also pretty. Large, green-yellow, with brown stems. There is much light, I see, I see the light for the first time, I actually *see* it. Light is good. The sun is good, it is a hazy, fiery yolk in the distance. A diagonal ray tickles my nose, I feel I'm going to sneeze and I giggle. I straighten the bib of my yellow, flowered overalls. I sit politely on a chair.

My younger, pudgy sister is in the playpen. She is also wearing overalls, white ones, and she is holding on to the rail, she wants to stand up. Today she is one year old. I do not look at her, I pay her no attention, my back is to the pen, I look at the sunray and the orchard. Everything is intensely colorful and pulses gently.

Mother comes from somewhere. MA-MA. She is not alone. She is carrying a neighbor's girl, the same age as my sister. Also pudgy, her milk-sister. Mother puts the neighbor girl in the carrier. Then she takes her camera out, snap snap. She asks us to look at her, to smile, she looks through the glass eye with a metal lid and shouts, shouts, my, how skinny and bony you are, darling, look at the two little babies, they are so chubby, so chunky, look at their red cheeks, why won't you eat? You're a big girl now, you're four years old and so skinny!

Snap snap, the camera. Ah, but . . . Somewhere, under the bib of the overalls, something breaks in two.

Oh, Mom. Someone removes her aerial hand from the top of my head. A dove's cooling flutter. I can feel it making me cold, something evil and black gapes open beneath my bib. A dark hole in the middle of my chest. I hate my younger sister, I hate both of those fat kids. And I don't understand. I want to cry, as usual, and I can't.

Something sad, very sad, a kind of fog gathers around me, in silence. As though there's no more sun; the orchard is snuffed out. I am choked by the bitter, black emptiness beneath my chest. I feel abandoned, like those nights when I have to sleep in my bed alone, but it's different. Something has broken. I don't understand. Something hurts. Between me and my mother, who is busy over the pen, there is an enormous, cold distance. Like a long and unfamiliar road, covered by mist and fog. Something hurts. I don't understand.

Mother leaves us to go inside the house. I turn and look. The two pudgy girls are out of the pen, my mother took them out. Now they are taking steps, rocking, silly-looking, their small legs akimbo. They are going toward the pump, which is dripping water. There is a gray metal tub where my mother does the laundry and washes us every night. The tub is full of water. Clear, cold water from the well. The pudgy girls are going toward the tub, they want to play with the water. They lean over the rim, sticking their chubby hands in the water. They slap it, they splash, they play, they like it. They giggle loudly. Then my sister wants to climb over the edge of the tub, which is fairly high, up to her chest. She can't. She begins to cry, her baby voice, her spoiled voice. She wants to get in the water. I see her round bottom in her white overalls, trying to climb into the tub. I have an idea. I look around, no one else is outside. I run toward the well, toward the tub. I grab my sister's overalls, I pick her up and drop her inside.

A large, white mark, covered with water. I see her sink to the bottom of the tub like a clump of earth. A mad joy flashes through me. I hear her screaming, loud, loud. Air bubbles come up to the choppy surface of the water. I run away, I duck behind a woodpile. I wait. After a few moments, Mother comes running out of the house. She looks toward the tub, she screams and grabs the pudgy girl out of the water. The pudgy girl wails, she cries hard, the water streams off of her. She drowns in tears, she stutters something between her gasps, makes motions. Mother takes here in her arms, dries her off, strokes her, kisses her, while her eyes search around her madly. She is trying to find me. Then she takes the two girls into the house.

I stare at the door for a few moments. I am not sorry. I have no regret. I am thinking of one thing only, one specific thing. I want to die. To disappear. I look around carefully, then I run down the street in front of the house. Toward the big, green park in the distance. The gravel crunches under my sandals.

Oh, Mother, why did you come, why did you take me out of that luxurious summer garden? Why did you show me other sisters, little sisters, mirrors, little mirrors? You took me and threw me to the other side, into the other garden, the one that was dark and too large. I heard a thin, silver thread snap above my head, snap in a high-pitched, soft sound, like the flutter of a dove spreading its wings, drawing its purple claws up to its body, quickly and mournfully rising beyond the clouds, into the deep sky. I felt a cosmic chill flood over me, it gathered around me like a corset, forever isolating me from you.

I go to the park, the place where my parents work, they leave in the morning and don't return until the evening. We live at the edge of the park, in a brick house, brown-ish-pink in color. The park is enormous, filled with trees and flowers. It has a long and strange name, and there are all kinds of paths, alleys, hidden spots. It has shady clutches of trees, two fields, and a lake surrounded by

reeds. And in the middle of the lake is an island and a cas-
tle with red-brick towers, where my mother and father
work. The large park is my playground, it belongs to me.
It is my kingdom from morning to evening. I know it like
I know the pockets of my overalls.

Now I run down a white gravel path, toward the field
of daisies. The daisies are tall this year, taller than I am, and
thick. From the edge of the field, I look at their long, green
stalks, leaning gently to the left, to the right. I watch them
with desire and attention. Somewhere, behind, there are
voices. Perhaps two grown people, a woman and a man.
I have to hide. I don't want them to see me. I want to be
alone, alone. I want to cry. I want to die. I don't want to be
in this world emptied of my mother.

I dart into the dogwood groves that grow around the
field, scraping my hands and legs slightly, but I don't care.
I walk carefully through the daisy stalks, pushing them
slowly to one side and the other. They are taller than I am,
their crowns come together over my head, I feel like I'm
in a magic grove, thick with light. Hard and furry green
stalks tickle the skin on my arms. From above, through
the few white petals, like long whale teeth, a light filters
down, and a salty smell from the pollen and pistils invades
me. The place is warm, scented, peaceful, without a buzz
to be heard, without a sound, only the crush of my steps
through the green stalks. I sit on the black earth, rough and

warm. I want to cry. I do, softly, in little sobs. I don't know why I'm crying, but I like it. I want to die. And it is okay.

And all at once, something happens to me. It is as though a weird heat comes from above and drugs me. I don't understand. It is as though a whiter light falls suddenly on the soft part of my head. Something surrounds me, melts over me, like a shower of cotton. At once I see the daisies more clearly than before, I don't know how, as though I am looking through a crystal that sharpens the outlines of the stalks and leaves and dyes them in prismatic colors. The daisies are large and alive, yes, alive, they nod in understanding, they watch me and they breathe. Then the large crown of a daisy leans down toward me, I see its round face, full of yellow seeds, it smells salty. Its yellow face, with a white halo of long, sparse petals, comes closer, it comes closer, it adheres to my face, it swallows me. I am suddenly inside a daisy. No, I become a daisy, a day-a-zee. I am white and green, my head is flat, and my face is a shining yellow, like a small sun surrounded by long teeth, white and sparse. I like it, I am tall, I rock from side to side. I feel beads of sweat under the four leaves that branch off me. I feel two black ants climbing up my green stalk, through the short, tough fur. The ants tickle me, I feel like laughing. I rock slowly to the right, to the left, in the heat of the morning, along with the entire field of daisies. I am not crying anymore, I feel content, reconciled. In the middle of the field, under the enormous avalanche of light, I am also a kind of light, with leaves, with blossoms, white-yellow-green, multiplied in countless daisy sisters. I am happy. I exist. I exist just as much as the field of daisies that goes far off in the distance.

Then I hear, from somewhere, from the edge of the field, a human voice, uh-oh, calling me by my girl name. For a moment, I don't recognize it. Oh, yes, it's my father, with a friend, a tall and haughty woman, a film director. They spotted me from far away, when I was hiding behind the living fence of dogwood in the little field. My father calls me again, half-heartedly, then I hear them walk off. I suddenly see my scraped knees, I marvel at my brown, misshapen sandals. I am back in my flowered overalls, a bit dirty. I remember everything, but I don't hurt anymore.

I want to stay here, I don't want to go back. Here, among the tall, green stalks, covered in fur, among the mute crowns of flowers rocking slowly, peacefully. I am suddenly very tired. I lie down among the flowers. On the black earth, rough and warm.

Oh, Mom, I am alone, I am in a forest. What is the forest like, my darling? It is a forest of tall, straight trees, a forest with sparse leaves and much light. I am walking by myself down a trail. What is the trail like, my love? The trail is pale and narrow, full of sand and little stones. There is no buzz, no birds around me, only the air rubbing leaves against each other, penetrated here and there by a blinding spear of sunlight. I'm holding a basket of food for Grandma. I find a tree fallen across the path. What is the tree like, dear? The tree is a thick and mighty oak, with branches full of leaves, golden bronze, deep veins. Bronze? Hm. Bronze. What are you doing next to the fallen tree? I'm thinking how to get over it, I don't know how at first, it's so thick, taller than I am. Then I look at its thick, beautiful branches, I break a big leaf off and put it inside my shirt, under the bib of my overalls. Then I think I might go around it, but in the end I climb through its twisted branches and clamber slowly over the thick trunk to the other side. I'm scraped up on my legs and arms, but I don't mind. I go farther, the path seems to have gotten wider in the meantime. What do you find next, little dove? I find a wild fruit tree, full of little yellow pears and caterpillars, too. What do you want to do? I want to clean off the caterpillars, like in the story. I pick one after another, they ring like your dangly earrings, as though they were plated with silver and blue and green stones. I put the caterpillars on a leaf, I pick a large yellow pear, I eat it, the sweet juice runs from my mouth, I wipe my face with my hand, I continue on my way.

A wolf appears. Are you afraid? Nooo, I'm not afraid. Well, I'm a little afraid, but I speak to the wolf calmly; I explain that I ran away from my home in the world, that I am not actually going to my grandmother's, and after a few moments of silence the wolf moves on. I continue down the trail, it's wider now and mottled with sunlight filtered through the wealth of leaves. On the side of the path, I see a mushroom with a large red cap, covered in little white dots. Are you thinking of picking it? Nooo, because you taught me they might be poisonous. On its domed hat I see a key. A key? Yes. What is the key like, my love? The key is small and old, but when I pick it up and rub it on the bib of my overalls, it turns into a large, bright key. It is gold, it has one end shaped like a clover, full of little precious stones, and it has three large teeth on the other end. Tell me, what will you do with the key? I stare at it hungrily, I clean it off and put it in the basket, on top of the food.

Then I move on. In the middle of the forest I find some running water. What is the water like, darling? It is a river, fairly wide, as wide as a field, but not deep, not navigable, I can see round, gray stones at the bottom. On the bank, I find a drinking glass. Yes? Yes. What is the glass like, dear? Describe it. The glass is simple, straight, no stem, like the ones you have in the kitchen, a little chipped at the lip, slightly cracked on one side. What do you do with the glass? I take it, wash out the dust, and use it to drink from the river. The water is good, it is cold, refreshing. Then, holding my sandals, I walk barefoot through the water, which only comes up to my knees. Aha! Goood! And what do you see on the other side? On the other side I see, far, far away, a house. A house? What's the house like? The house is tall and white, there's a balcony on the second story, and the front door is half-open. It looks like our brick house beside the park, but empty. Long uninhabited. Abandoned. I don't like it, I don't know why, but I'm scared, I go near the house but not inside it, I look at it from the trail. I don't like the half-open door, full of shadows, through it I can see part of a strange backyard, full of a slanted blue light. It seems you are there, hidden behind the door, dressed in dark clothes. You call me, you tempt me, but I don't come. I want to stay in the luminous forest, on the white gravel path.

Oh, Mother, mortal gorgon, enormous medusa, bitter-sweet pain, from my childhood heaven you gaze at me directly, you focus on me, you watch over me. You, the woods where I once awoke, lucid and alone. You, the thick, red water I once only barely escaped, which I fear to approach, because I think I'll try to drown myself. Why do you scare me, popping out of forgotten apartments, rusted mirrors, old wardrobes with half-open doors? In your long gown, you wait for me, silently, in the last room, there where I enter in fear, shaking with horror, yet also joy, looking for the door, the gate, the narrow shadowy passage toward the yard. The luminous yard. Oh, Mother, why won't you leave, why do you stay in the house so long?

Awakened from her sleep, again and again, the child rubs her wet, drowsy eyes and cries without a cause. She cries because she was extracted from the ancestral void and her existence begun, she was suddenly brought into this incomprehensible life, she cries just because she breathes and feels, she doesn't yet know what, why, to what purpose, for what point, in light of what. A strange brilliance awoke before her eyes, an atavistic fear. She intuited vaguely that she would live, against her will; once wrenched without her permission from the vast, anonymous substrate, she would have to live through terrible trials of growth, reproduction, decline, crucifixion, and disappearance. The way an enormous thought, in order to exist in this world, must descend, from all its star-covered endlessness in the woman's tight womb, and pass through the terrible humiliations of birth, full of blood, amniotic fluid, and torn and tortured flesh, then through the servitude of being raised, with the discipline of feeding, washing, and dressing, through the continual filthiness of excrement, infection, and all types of illness, through the trauma of schooling, with tears, pain, weariness, sweat, the suffering of encounters with individuals different from or similar to ourselves, encounters full of attraction, envy, love, hate, pity, horror, through the humiliation of carnal degradation, aging, and weakening, and then through the pains of final crucifixion, with the shame of fear, loss of control, urination, cold sweats, with the helplessness of inescapable despair, and at the end of everything, the humiliation of death. And of whatever there is to come.

The more-than-worldly greatness of this enormous thought will have to shrink itself to the point of annihilation, concentrate itself into a single point, a protean cell, in order to enter the terrestrial proliferation of stuff, will, slowly-slowly, morula-blastula-gastrula, have to grow, to multiply, to construct itself by deconstructing, by destroying itself, and then renew itself and die again, without end. It will have to make eyes—to wake from sleep, to study ridiculous, useless things, to understand primitive, barbarous things. To suffer, to be cruel, to enjoy, to lose itself and to find itself in all kinds of temptations and trials, and to lose itself again, and to find itself again. From the star-covered endlessness, to pass through strange metamorphoses, to be a point, a minuscule seed, egg, worm, larva, fetus, then an infant, child, pubescent, adolescent, young woman, mature woman, old woman, and in the end, a corpse. To be everything, to then be nothing, to become something primitive but possible, then something evolving yet grotesque, and maybe sometime something extraordinarily beautiful, almost star-like, something almost endless, something cosmic, and then to be again nothing. To withstand diminution, annihilation, to risk losing itself again in the absolute, in order to animate a bit of dust, a bit of sweat, a bit of careless matter, and then to recover itself, with a bit of luck, from death.

And the replicas of this misunderstood masochism to become incarnate in millions of species of bacteria and animals, in millions of insects, fish, birds, mammals, in millions of forms of horns, wings, hooves, reproductive organs, in millions of forms of slithering, fluttering, shrieks and cries, millions of times and in millions of examples. Filling the already packed atmosphere of this small, strange planet with their agitations, frightened, comic, excited, famished, ridiculous, and worthy of vast pity and enormous tenderness. An immeasurable and overwhelmingly tender pity, from which springs an enormous question, in response to the initial, enormous thought, springs like an impetuous and revolted geyser

over the planetary sphere of garbage, blood, organic substances, and gases, that question we must animate, and
feed, and transform with our lives: my God, my great
God, why was all this necessary?

MUST

Darling, I must tell you stories. I must discharge my strange visions. This interior sea that almost drowns me, where atolls of brilliant orange coral surface from time to time. But why do only certain moments *bother us, return to us, electrify our memory? The rest is only ballast, anonymous residue, kilometers of gray film stock, decomposed, veiled in our fragmented memory, scattered, confused. Why do only certain scenes insist on returning to our minds, out of the enormous, vague storehouse of the past, since only irresistible flashes come to us? Some moments do matter, some emanate a certain aura, a vibration, they illuminate a certain invisible field of emotional power. And these moments are few. And surprising, and unexpected, because they are not those that might seem important to our exterior selves, our social roles, which we share with others in the theater we act in together. Memories important to others are never the same as our own; each of our essential memories is unique, although they do have something obscure and important in common with other people's. And these moments, for each of us, lack any clear* thread. And they often lack even a connection with all our sufferings and loves and dramas, viewed from the outside. They have only, as I was telling you, an interior illumination, a strange emotional power. One that pulses within them inexhaustibly, like an energy of another nature, whenever—by mistake, most often—a detail, a smell, a taste, a strange sound, an intense color pulls them from their neuronal lethargy and activates the mysterious synapses that let them play over our mental screen. They are like radioactive rocks of uranium and strontium, poking their glimmering corners out of the inner ocean—an ocean that can be agitated or apathetic. But all the other moments, days, years are only a dark dross, only ash.

Darling, I must, I must remember these moments, I must tell you their stories, because in some way that I do not understand and cannot erase, they endowed the core of my being within me, they nourished me, they transformed me. I must strive to fish them out of the flavorless and inchoate ocean of existence. Which is nothing more than a disorganized preparation, a prolonged wait, like a tide of sea trash that comes in and out; it is the lukewarm, steaming compost from which these sparse moments erupt, like sumptuous flowers that never wither. Withstanding these strange, intense moments is not as easy as it looks. Sometimes it is an almost nauseating strain, other times it is electrifying, almost ecstatic. As though I were infected with a psychic or mental energy beyond my capacities, one that frightens my body.

I wish I could line these moments up end to end, only these experiences, perhaps not more than a few days all in all, and which constitute, in sum, my true life. *Through which I feel* something *is transmitted, through my life or any other. Something that does not have to do with me alone, the richness of those moments coming from the depths and the heights does not belong to me, just as the sky does not belong to me, or the waters of the sea. What remains of time is a certain unclear, foggy, dormant film. I must reconstruct, in detail, a handful of sensations that exceed the scale, a series of expanded perceptions, strange states between waking and sleeping and super-wakefulness, amazing coincidences, the sum, in the end, of everything I have truly* experienced. *Or that which something has experienced through me. A state. A lucidity. A presence. Another being or, better put, another form of being, yet tied to me. Like a second consciousness, wider, vaster, that wants to be born, to appear in the world.*

These are the moments when I was, *when I* awoke. *But what I* awoke *to is difficult to explain. There is a strange emotional fissure between my interior worlds, an elliptical memory, a vertiginous mental spiral, a Möbius strip, which I have yet to comprehend. Because as present as they are in themselves, these moments outpace my intelligence, and they frighten me. And as vivid as they are, they remain enigmatic. As though by mistake I reached a* dangerous *zone, unknown, but not prohibited. Something that is at hand but unknown. As though I leaped unprepared into another level of my being that I thought was locked away. As though I walked into a lavish interior film that outpaces my imagination. And, in this film, I only intentionally participated in a few disparate scenes, without understanding the entire script. I went as though by chance to the other side, into the supersensorial fields. Into the world of vibrant, vital, essential images. As though by some chance I ran into myself, the complete me at last, the real me at last, a more subtle creature, vaster and more impersonal, within a world outside of time and truer than the world we call real. Something that waits within everyone and manifests in all those who are able to experience it.*

THE FIRST ENLIGHTENMENT

1

I am almost thirteen years old. I am at a school summer camp in Transylvania, it's a hazy, hot summer morning in August. All the students are waiting in the hall of the main camp building, in the deafening buzz of hundreds of boys' and girls' voices, then we go to the music room and practice the songs for the closing ceremony. I feel a sudden, odd pressure in my womb, as though there's something heavy and dense inside, a piece of metal shot. A hole in my womb and a cold sweat fill me with panic. I slip quickly out of the room, before our portly, bald music teacher arrives. I run to hide somewhere, the basement, maybe the gym.

I can see what's coming. It will last an hour, with the precision of an invisible clock, as it has at the start of every month for the past six months; I will suffer through atrocious pains in my lower stomach, so strong I think I'll die, or simply lose my mind. After an hour, the pains will pass, as though they had never been.

The unsettling pressure begins again. I'm afraid I won't get below in time, to the basement. I run down the wide stone stairway, but the blow strikes my stomach suddenly, ineluctably. A rhythmic pulse, a pitiless and burning metronome, rises slowly from my pubis. A wave of heat and sweat crosses over me. The pains rise slowly, like invisible water, through the porous tissue of my abdomen. My vision goes dark, I am in darkness. I am somewhere deep, I don't know where, I don't know who I am, my consciousness is completely focused on a single, intense point, full of panic. I can't think of anything but that point, obsessively, to withstand the terrible pain. It comes rhythmically, in waves, like a tide that reaches its culmination in the center of my body, then retreats, pauses, and comes back again. The pain approaches like an evil force, an enemy; it attacks me, it lays siege to my single point of conscious thought, focuses on itself in my stomach, as though it wants to destroy me. I feel trapped inside a deep cavern, in an unlit area underground, where I must pass through some primitive trial, I have to withstand something difficult, as painful as crucifixion, like being pierced with arrows, and if I don't, I die, I disintegrate. The pains come in dense, dark waves. I focus desperately on the pain, on its sharpest point, in the internal matrix of my stomach. I feel I must think the pain, to move it to my mind, to visualize it in front of my closed eyes, or I will not withstand it. I mold its viscous and frightening substance into all kinds of contorted, bizarre shapes, spheres and tubes, bacteria and viruses, like those I saw through the microscope in Biology, twitching their soft matter, red-brown and dark. Larvae and snakes, crocodiles and platypuses, all kinds of creatures slither past my mind, I shape them with my thoughts, then I crush them with hatred, with desperation. Lizards, buzzards, rats, then voracious mammals, carnivores, tigers and lions and panthers attacking sheep, oxen, and giraffes, I tear all their aggressive or ridiculously delicate shapes to shreds. In my mind I am bathed in blood and hatred. My mind is a dark cavern, the site of barbarous, pitiless carnage. At the same time, I feel my skin covered in sweat.

I find myself suddenly in a violent sea, full of a wet and viscous matter, brownish-red in color. I see a bare, pointed rock in the middle of the heavy, breaking waves. I throw myself onto the cold, bitter metal rock, with all my mind, with all my will. From that place, with an almost painful lucidity, I see a tiny, luminous point, barely visible in the distance. Across the heavy, magnetic waves, the point comes quickly, quickly toward me. Its light is more and more intense, more brilliant, and, like a minuscule sun, it enters my chest gone mad with pain and brings it calm. In a moment I see myself from without. I see how, as I fled toward the basement, I fell down the stone stairway and my soft body slid down the steps, headfirst, my skirt pulled up, all a mess. I am beside my body, beside myself, slightly above. I stare as it, my pain-racked adolescent body, slides down the stairs, like a stupid doll, pulled apart, and I whisper calmly, decisively, "Keep your head up, or you'll break your neck! Keep it up!"

I find myself at the bottom of the stone stairs. I am balled up into myself, my knees are pulled almost to my mouth, I look like a bruised fetus, brutally expelled from a cold and pitiless uterus, one as wide as the basement where I am. The pains slowly retreat, gently, as though the black-brown water were tamed, it goes back down like a warm and salty wave, into the point in my stomach from which it burst. Exhausted, like after a fierce battle with a merciless, terrible force, I ask myself in wonder: why, for what? Why must I suffer so much? What kind of trial must I pass through each month? It's as though I've died and risen, as though I've fallen into a chasm and climbed out, as though I have conquered a wild and immense force. Now I am eased and purified. Then I feel a tiny sphere, red and burning, leave me, below, between my legs.

2

I leave the main camp building, I take the long path toward the wooden cabins that house the beds. I am extremely tired, I absolutely must lie down, must rest. I have to cross a low part of the path, under high, dark branches that watch over the straight gravel walkway. I am cold, and the distant rustling branches give me chills and a certain anxiety. Down the path in the blue distance, I see a thin, gangly shadow approaching. It's a boy, a fact that makes me suddenly irritated. Recently, whenever I come near any boy I feel a kind of negative, evil energy rising over my legs and arms, making me tremble for no reason. I brace myself, remind myself I will pass him as I usually do, without looking up. I inhale deeply. The shadow comes closer, he is dressed in something white, a sweater, I think, thick yarn. I can't resist glancing at him from the corner of my eye as he passes, while he pretends he is not looking at me. He is a tall boy, gangly and brown-haired, with the start of a short, black mustache, which makes a nice contrast with the white of his sweater.

And in that moment, something happens to me. It's like I was struck gently in the soft spot on my head. I feel a mildly luminous warmth invade me through the top of my head and descend in a flash to the tips of my toes. For a moment, I feel paralyzed. It's like I am waking from sleep, from a kind of torpor, and I see myself much better, more clearly. I see the chubbiness and pudginess in my body now, and I don't like it, not at all, the way I'm standing, still and ridiculous, thunderstruck, in the middle of the path, trying to understand what is happening to me. The boy has passed already, I hear his footsteps clearly moving away, firm and plodding down the fine gravel. But I cannot move because I see and hear everything with an unreal clarity and intensity. I see every piece of gravel on the ground, with its particular details, blue, gray, pink, rose, and black, with gold and silvery points, with irregular shapes, but which seem so—how to put it—meaningful, with little shadows between their edges and curves, shadows now so full of a pulsating life. The branches around me seem alive and attentive, they are a kind of green presence, a rustling expressiveness, vibrating on each side of the path; it's as though every tree that stands silently were a unique person, of a select nobility, trying to contact me; the motions of its branches draw an intelligent and mysterious message on the air. My scent has also awoken, it has its own intense existence, and it enjoys the dizzying tree sap, the mild smell of white blossoms beside the path, the aroma of dry stones warmed in the sun. My hearing perceives the ever softer crush of the gravel under the calm footsteps in the distance. I am completely here, on this path, in this strange and dilated moment that holds me prisoner in its transparent sphere, in its invisible hermetic bubble. I cannot think of any one thing, I am all attention, I am conscious of all that is happening to me, and I feel that warm luminosity still in my chubby, ridiculous body, a body which for the first time is truly seeing itself.

I know, however, without putting it into words, in the depths of my instinct, which the pains of my abdomen have just liberated, that this state is connected to the shadow that disappeared.

3

In the days that followed, I would encounter that gangly boy many times, always in his white sweater of thick yarn. His name was Radu, and he was from a different provincial town than I was. He was about two years older than me, and he seemed the tallest of his crowd of boys, because I could always spot him easily, at any distance, wherever he was. And whenever I thought I saw his unmistakable white sweater, my heart would beat wildly. It would pound so awfully against my ribs that I was afraid it would burst through. From time to time, the beat would flutter and practically make me faint. I was sick, I was nauseous, I was so scared my blood froze in my arteries and veins, my chest became painful and rigid, as it began to round up into breasts. It was as though something inside me became scared to death by the sight of his gangly shadow. It was as though something unknown inside me furiously opposed something else, as it began to grow there. The energy I received on seeing him seemed too intense, too alien for my poor internal organs and members; they had just begun to grow, to transform, they were frightened by the far-reaching, unbearable electric shock. If I had to walk past Radu, on a path or in the cafeteria, I felt I would fall over; or when he glanced at me, observed me, saw me, I felt I would disappear, pure and simple, although in the end nothing happened at all, and he didn't pay me any attention.

Instead, as could have been expected, I started to speak in verse and to write poetry. I found myself perorating in rhyme to my roommates, who were used to the quiet girl I had been. Inspiration struck most often at night. After the other girls had gone to bed, I would open the dorm room window, climb onto the wide oak window frame, gaze at the stars through the telescope I made with my hands, and start to make quiet sounds—often without knowing exactly what I was saying, sometimes it felt as though my mouth produced phrases that did not belong to me, they surprised me such that they seemed to belong to another being awakening within me, a more intelligent being, more complete. I sang about the sun and the planets, about our solar system and the Milky Way, using what I had learned in school, but *differently*, I don't know how, with another understanding, with another emotion, as though I could fill myself with something alive and vast, something boundless that freed me from myself and took me beyond the contours of my body.

One night, after all the other girls were asleep, I crawled through the window and up onto the roof. I had discovered that the attic door wasn't locked, and a short, rickety wooden ladder led to the gently angled roof of the cabin. Lying lazily on the tin still warm from the day's sunlight, I gazed aimlessly at the night and stars, thousands of stars like a white dust of ground glass. I thought of nothing. I looked at the dark. The simple fact that I had climbed up there—where no one could find me, where I could be all alone with myself and my heart awakening to life—filled me with a feeling of complete freedom, of vastness, of deep happiness. I was empty of thoughts, dissolved in the soft darkness, the velvety blue-black, illumined weakly by scattered stars and constellations, cut across by night birds, scored by falling stars.

The night is deep, is warm. No sound reaches me

from below, the branches do not rustle, the crickets do not chirp. It is a calm silence, immense, filled with peace. In a moment, I become aware of the dense presence of silence, as though it is full of something limitless, alive, and also aware. I feel somehow fed by this profound, almost intelligent silence. Something birdlike, delicate, a downpour of fine particulates filters through my skin, into my veins and arteries. I feel perfectly insulated from the rest of the world, wrapped in a cocoon of birdlike batting, I am in the magical center of the world, and at the same time dissolved into the sweet darkness, one with the limitless night. And in a moment, slowly, I begin to hear a song, a music. A strange music, barely noticeable yet clear, crystalline. I lift myself onto my elbows and look around me. It is a kind of song, simple but harmonious; it reminds me of music boxes and their naïve, childlike sounds. But what I hear now is a vast music, from a music box as large as the scene that surrounds me, as large as the entire world. It seems to come from every direction, on the waves of night breezes, or to descend from the stars. Something sweet, swaying, like silver bells, sounding in unison, then separately, following each other and climbing each other to dizzying sonorous heights, then falling in quick cascades, in grave, vibrant eddies, then rising again, uniting again in the peaks of glittering jingling, in unison like a chorus of a thousand whispering fairies, sprites, and spirits, then separating in ramified chords of an immense, invisible organ. Something both gentle and encompassing descends over the earth, something full of a vast goodness, something loving, and incomprehensible.

The song—the thought passes through my mind—seems to come from a clocktower; I lie unmoving and listen closely, amazed: could I be near one of those old, medieval clocks with silly mechanical figures that move rigidly, at odd angles, to a simple and monotone song, every half hour or hour? But there are no such towers in our camp. Next I think maybe the façade of the main camp building has a large clock with a white porcelain face and a music machine. Up to now I've never seen or heard it, but, who knows, maybe tonight someone turned it on. But, I remember quickly, musical clocks like that usually play patriotic songs, waltzes, or marches that everyone knows. The song I'm hearing now is not familiar, but its melody and harmony are well played. It is calming, clear, and it does not seem to come from a precise direction. It is crystalline and comes from everywhere, it is like a sonorous sublimation of the night, its gentle and limitless calm arrives from afar and from long ago, and yet from beside me, from very close. It encompasses me, it covers me like the embrace of the consciousness of the summer sky, I think to myself, in fact it thinks in myself; it exists as a kind of understanding in my mind, suddenly calm, crystalline, like a pristine mirror reflecting the surrounding night, like a new organ of perception. But it is music, actually music, it is a harmonious song, not the whistling wind, not the rustling branches, not the chirping insects. And it is not my imagination; I look at myself, I am awake, on the roof, holding my arms in the cold.

There is something beatific in this surprising song. I let it soak into me, its diaphanous harmonies fill my mind with the image of a giant celestial clock, full of wheels, gears, balls, and bars, which in fact are galaxies, solar systems, and planets, with their satellites, meteors, and comets, all turning in circles and ellipses, sliding, rising, and falling across vertiginously tilted planes, along complicated spirals, producing the audible harmonious sounds. I listen ravenously, in exhilaration. Then, bit by bit, like a gentle breeze, like a wave of vibrations retreating slowly into the warm matrix of the dark, the birdlike music goes away, slowly ceases. After waiting in the cold, in the tension of my sense of hearing, I decide to stop listening, I give in to my tiredness and slowly climb down from the roof.

The next day, I ask the other girls if they heard something while our room window was open. They did not. I ask the teacher in charge of our group if there is a musical clocktower in the camp. There is not. I think then maybe someone had been messing around with a church clock-tower, but I learn that there is no church nearby.

The next night I go back on the roof. But the music does not repeat. I wait patiently. Nothing. Long past midnight, very tired, I climb down. The third night, I climb up again, even though my hopes have fallen, and I am starting to think it was a vision, or better put, an *audition*. This time I bring a blanket with me, so I won't be cold as morning comes. I wait. I wait. I hear nothing but the soft, resigned rustle of the branches around me, and the tenacious, mechanical chirping of the insects. I look at the stars and their dust of crushed glass. Nothing else happens.

On the fourth night, I did not climb back onto the roof. I stayed in the room, waited for the girls to fall asleep, then I climbed up and sat on the window frame, and there, without going farther, I looked at the stars. I sang softly, dangling my thin legs, I gazed ravenously at the black-blue mountain sky, filled with tiny pearls, crystals, and diamonds, as though the skin of a drum pierced by countless holes, through which shining threads of milk flowed, from the ocean of light beyond. My small brain struggled to understand what "infinite" meant, where the end of the universe was, what the earth was in this sea of stars, and what I was, a girl, a minuscule being, a kind of intelligent microbe, as I learned at school, a kind of unsteady red globule of blood inside a cell, itself part of a wide tissue in a giant body, on this giant planet. I imagined the red globule intensely, I liked this image, it fascinated me, I played with it intensely in my mind. And I do not know how, *I do not know how*, I was absorbed into my mind; the red cell exited through the top of my head and I found myself suddenly somewhere high, in the heights of the night, outside the terrestrial atmosphere, in the space between the planets. I floated like a little sphere in a warm, welcoming, elastic darkness. I left the earth behind, an Easter egg painted with a lot of blue, a little yellow-ochre, and dark green, an ever smaller egg, ever farther away. I drifted tranquilly past the moon, with its puffy, red face, like a young girl crying, praying, and begging, always begging for something, some particular thing, from her terrestrial mother. I spun vertiginously toward the sun, which pulled me like the fire of a total, measureless love, I passed through it rapidly in an enormous, terrifying roar, like an oven that had melted light down to its incandescence, then I spun spectacularly to the right and left of our solar system. I turned now with a dizzying speed toward the center of the Milky Way, through thousands of other solar systems, each shining like strands of pearls in the vast and spacious void, but, I do not know how, I turned again to the right and departed the gray-white plane, domed like a lens, of the galaxy. I turned toward my initial target, toward the end of the universe, toward the end of the end, because I wanted to know the limit of the infinite and what something that cannot be thought might mean. I tried to condense myself into a singular point, the central point, and at the same time to make my thinking-presence fill all the universes, all the abysses. And again I traveled with a dizzying speed and passed through innumerable solar systems, and yet I did not get anywhere. At a certain moment, I thought that everything was just repeating, as though I had been moving in circles or spirals, on a twisted double loop, because whatever I saw first on my right would appear next on my left, or what I saw above me was later below, like a silent cosmic dance with large, intersecting geometric figures I could not decipher. And at a certain moment I became tired, I stopped and saw before me a strange hieroglyph levitating over the dark abyss: a large figure eight, horizontal, burning red in color, attached at one end to another horizontal figure eight, also red. An infinity sign in the mouth of another infinity sign. And at that moment I understood. Infinity raised to infinity still equals infinity, infinity squared or cubed or raised to any power always equals infinity, the same prime, initial, infinity. The universe has no beginning, no end. It is like a double twisted loop that contains its own initial point and everything that follows. And however many infinities I would exceed, I would always find myself inside the same initial infinity, continuously swallowing its starting point, the matrix, the origin, consuming itself in its innumerable twists, like a thought that eternally emits and devours itself, repeating itself, multiplying itself to infinity. And this double infinity, like a red mouth kissing a matching mouth, is alive and loves and wants to be understood and loved.

I find myself back again suddenly, on the oak window frame of the dorm room. I do not know how I broke out and I do not know how I returned. I felt a minuscule spinning, like an eddy, in the middle of the top of my head. In my eyes, I still have that strange sign, burning red, two horizontal figure eights gripping each other, only much smaller in my mind, and much paler. Above my head, I can see the deep ocean of the dark and the stars and, at the bottom, me, a little fish in the great aquarium of the earth, in my white, flowered nightshirt. Almost asleep, I move toward my bed.

4

Radu somehow heard I liked him. The other boys probably told him, teasing him about the way my face changed
when I saw him. Or maybe a jealous girl drew his attention to my ridiculous poetess-y behavior. But Radu did
not pay me one bit of attention, and I was in no shape to
overcome my inhibitions when I saw him. One morning,
however, I was in a group of girls and boys that had gathered around the flagpole in the main camp yard while
we waited for our meal. It did not take long for Radu to
arrive, and the other boys greeted him quickly and happily. I was back to one side of the group, trying not to
look at him and not to show any of the intense emotions
that undulated through my silly, pudgy body and wiped
away any coherent thought. At a certain moment, there
was a quick and strange motion among the boys, after
they had been whispering something, and I don't know
how but I found myself next to Radu, in the middle of a
wide circle around the flagpole, as the other kids moved
back and looked at us, giggling among themselves. I knew
that Radu was not paying attention to me, and that my
awkwardness could do nothing but amuse him. I knew
that the other boys were mean and loved nothing more
than to bait the girls, to make them suffer, to laugh at
them. And yet there I was next to Radu, and I couldn't do

anything but stand powerless in this ridiculous moment, unable to move. Because I was next to him, next to Radu, and that filled me with a strange, unspoken feeling, something sweet. Without being able to raise my eyes toward him, I felt his presence, like a magnetic warmth that drew me closer with insidious force, stronger than my will, and filled me little by little with an unexpected joy. I could see everything out of the corner of my eye, how the kids in the circle held their hands over their mouths to keep from laughing, I saw the yellow, sandy ground around the flagpole, the white sneakers and khaki pants Radu had on, but I didn't care. I could feel something happening deep inside me, something more interesting than anything else in the world. The sun across the bolt of heaven bathed our young, raw heads in heat, but through Radu I discovered another kind of sun. My short, chubby body, the one I had so hated up to then, suddenly appeared worthy of love, because it hid an unknown warmth inside, a tiny sun that began to vibrate, communicating silently with the tiny sun inside Radu's body and with the giant sun outside.

Then I raised my eyes slowly and looked directly above, toward the sky. The sun let itself be seen, it was not unbearable, it was not blinding as I had expected, rather it was, how to put it, it was welcoming, caressing, I looked at it for a long time, right in its face. And entering through my pupil, a calm, vast joy overtook me. I felt the projection of the faraway globe of fire inside me, I felt it plunging into my chest, mirroring itself there, in my chest, like in a hand mirror. And in that moment, a kind of invisible thread stretched between the sun and me. It was a loving umbilical cord; a warm and good liquid flowed down this pipe and connected us. For a moment I had the impression that I had somehow gone into the sun, that I had catapulted myself softly into its heart and filled its center with myself, I encompassed it from within. We shaped something together, a luminous and illuminating whole. A gentle explosion of interior light filled me and expanded me. A kind of burning gold caressed me from within, and I felt limitless. Something like an illuminating glory is what I felt emanating from me, something like a luminous warmth spread from my body to my surroundings. A vibration, full of goodness, made me one with all I saw; I felt waves full of the love of beings and things around me. In the silence that fell over my mind, in the silence that seemed to fill the entire world, I was completely happy, I was completely reconciled.

That is how I first knew Adoration.

DARLING

Darling, don't think I'm going crazy, or leading you down the garden path. I'm like you, normal enough, I do my part, like everyone, since I can't do anything else; I get up at seven thirty every morning, go to work, talk a little politics with my coworkers, leaf through the fashion magazines, appliance ads, newspapers, I go shopping, pay my bills, cook, watch a little TV in the evenings, sometimes read a bit before falling asleep, and I often dream. But from time to time, I am assaulted by strange images, powerful ones, charged with bizarre, excessive energy, visions that seem to climb out of unknown depths within me, or they come from above, from an interior heaven of the mind or someplace farther away. They speak a language other than our consonants and vowels and logical connections and punctuation. In fact, they do not speak, they only indicate, they show—they show and fall silent. They do not seem to be from our concrete, material world, which refuses the penetration of their strange energy, their soft electricity. They come from somewhere else, and yet, and yet, they have a connection with what is profound and vital; before the eyes of the mind, they create a certain dance, an enigmatic undulation, like an inner aurora borealis, that occasionally rustles the curtains of sense in the center of the brain. We ought to understand something of this mental undulation, to unravel an enigma, to let ourselves be carried, taken higher, transformed by a rejuvenating energy, we ought to accept something like a quantum leap, like enlightenment. Why these special images do not use our simple and clear logic of yes and no, full and empty, day and night, this and that, our everyday, domestic, linear logic of good and evil, black and white, feminine and masculine—I do not know, darling, I cannot say. Sometimes, this strange logic of theirs drives me crazy, it exasperates me. Maybe because I should understand these images in another way, with a different mind than the ordinary one I have. With an expanded mind, which, alongside the body and senses and reason, should include vision and imagination and sur-reason. A mind amplified above and below and in all directions, a mind with its axons of innumerable neurons extended to the center of the earth and its dendrites unrolled up to the stars, a mind that encompasses both our vast interior and the planet as well.

THE SECOND ENLIGHTENMENT

1

I saw Radu again three years later, at the same Transylvanian summer camp. Radu was unchanged, he still wore the same raggedy white sweater that showed off his black hair and gangly profile; maybe he was a little taller. I had changed more than he had, I was not as chubby, boys were giving me looks, but I was just as shy and withdrawn. We ran into each other along the same tree-lined path, where, spying his unmistakable profile from far away, I began to tremble again for no reason, an atavistic fear invaded me. Radu recognized me and stopped to talk, he seemed pleased. He told me about his literary successes in some provincial high-school magazines, about his passion for the German romantics and reincarnation. He talked a lot, he talked quickly, and he stared at me fixedly, and loomed over me in a way; he wanted to impress me, to show that he understood girls, and he did make an impression. We saw each other a few more times, in various groups of friends, in various locations in the camp, he always talkative while I fell into long silences, speechless with the avalanche of feelings that blocked my mouth, my breathing, my mind.

During one of the afternoons, we went out for a walk together in the forest beside the camp. I knew that Radu could not love me, I knew this in a sort of diffuse way, but deeply and definitively. Although being around him made me suffer terribly, with a trembling that filled me with fear, sometimes with horror, it also attracted me with a powerful force, to which I could only submit, as though to an implacable, irreversible decision, because in it I could sense, I do not know how, an unexpected possibility for my being, an escape from limitation, a dizzying openness.

Now we are on a walk in the woods; he stops talking, I stop talking. It is very quiet, there is nothing to hear, no sound. Not even rustling leaves, no whistling birds, no chirping insects, at least, that was how it seemed to me. The thought passes through my mind that a silence like this is strange, in a forest of pines and beech trees. Everything seems to have stopped. No bird. No sign of wind. No movement. Complete silence. Too complete, eerie. I suddenly slip into this strangeness, and although Radu's presence makes my body tremble constantly, like an almost unbearable electric current is passing through me, all my senses are acute, and my mind is working very quickly. Unstoppable rivers of images flow through my mind. I do not know how this intense vision invades me, but it fills my internal screen. The vision of a world in which there are only two beings, the two of us—two teenagers—him and me. I experience the broad and disturbing image of a world filled with vegetation, a luxurious, fantastic vegetation, of a deep, succulent green, but without any beings aside from us. The two of us, created directly onto the planet. A boy and a girl, two teenagers lost somehow, driven away from someplace, who drifted away from the road, among enormous, millennial trees with thick, contorted trunks, under the shadowy dome of leaves pierced with sun, in a deep, complete silence. This feeling overwhelms me with its majesty, strangeness, and loneliness.

I know that this vast, eerie vision, charged with a certain power, persisting on my retina as long as I am walking, this vision is connected to the fact that Radu is beside me, and I want to know why it is happening to me and not to him, too. I ought to take his hand and I cannot. I ought to move toward him, to press my body against his and I cannot. My excessive ardor beside his detached cool. My presence beside his absence. A nonmeeting, an absence, a distance. That is where the planet's magical loneliness comes from. Its barrenness seems horrifying to me, its fearful and sacred greatness. I tremble, it is more than I can stand. I depart from the vision and return in a moment with great confidence, like a kind of tenderness given from outside, I return as though to a lavish gift, to the fact that I hear birds whistling again, and the forest is full of insects and animals. Beasts, large and small and minuscule, other than ourselves, the two human cubs wandering off the road, all these species fluttering, howling, burrowing, munching, chirping all around us. I suddenly understand their existence as a beneficence, a salvation, because they prove the world may be other than it appears. Because they show what we have inside, and what we have yet to know or to recognize is given to us, presented from outside. The beasts pour out from forests within us.

The barren planet returns to my mind, it is a particularly forceful thought-vision, I plunge into it again hungrily, with a gravity beyond my years, even a slightly frightened exhilaration, as though I've stumbled upon something important. I understand, somehow, with a different and unlimited understanding, that people in general, represented at this moment by the two of us in this silent forest, are small gods, but blind, forgetful, egotistical. I understand something valuable, but it is not clear, not limpid; we are actually small gods but also children, infant gods, created by a greater force, planted here in a vast, receptive uterus, thrown into the loneliness of a planet of immense, impersonal power, in order to grow and to understand. To conclude our unconcluded being and to transform into something, into something else. We are seeds sown into the brown-black loam of a terrestrial existence, and we must germinate and rise slowly from our fragile burgeoning, our green sprouting, through layers of clay and stone, through bacteria, worms, and insects that wish to devour us, we must pierce through sheets of underground water and enemy root systems, our germinations are deviated by contrary forces, deceived by gravitations and visions, by temptations and traps, but pulled upward by an atavistic, core instinct, along a fragile thread of light, pulled by an inverted, celestial gravity, we are tractable, attracted toward growth at any price, driven to rise in spite of the avalanches of danger and difficulty, in spite of weakness, suffering, decay, gnashing our teeth, weeping, suffering, opening our exterior eyes first, then the eye of the heart, then the eye of the mind, to proceed through the crust of the planet toward the true light, toward the sun.

But how many seeds do grow tenaciously toward the true sun? I depart from my vision again, I feel Radu beside me, silent, and I let the image of the barren planet slowly-slowly leave me, this time completely. And I give thanks again, in my thoughts, for the fact that we have not been left completely alone in the world, in this enormous genetic sack, like a multitude of *I*'s that do not love *you*, like a *we* that does not love *you*, but instead we are surrounded by beings of many types and shapes, both visible and unseen, beautiful and repulsive, impossible and ridiculous, monstrous and amazing, creatures that the fertile planet imagined in other geological, biological, or psychological ages, perhaps in its childhood, perhaps in its adolescence, with all of its hormonal aggression and aberration, innumerable and patient creatures meant to exhaust all its emotional and morphological powers, to embody all the states of anger, reverie, and nightmare, to accompany us, to embody something and to help us to leave something behind. To awaken us, in the end. To remind us. To help us *understand*. But understand what, exactly?

2

I saw Radu again much later, completely by chance. I was at a huge party at the architecture students' club, when, in a group of people arriving late, I spotted a dark-haired man, whose long, gangly profile reminded me of something. He was with a blond-haired woman, it was clear they were together from the way they held hands and stood together quietly. Still, something in the person of that unknown man intrigued me; staring at him, I felt a hidden and forgotten mechanism began to whir inside of me, like a bow suddenly released, a spring, mysterious, because a certain sweet-warm heat stole into me behind my sternum. The heat reminded me of a particular state, something I had long forgotten. I tried to figure out what was attracting and disturbing me, at the same time that I pretended to pay attention to conversation and sipped slowly from a glass of red Martini and lemon, but, after a spell, when I had almost stopped thinking of that disturbing, discomforting sensation, I suddenly understood, I remembered. And I was taken up in a violent and joyful nostalgia, as though I had come out of a dark prison to find a night sky full of stars. Late that evening, at home alone, after trying to sleep for a long time, tossing and turning in sheets that felt too warm, I had this dream:

An old scholar, a venerable savant, speaking to a group of young people, invisible women and men whom I do not see but feel around me, protests the practice of autopsy. In an emotional, baritone voice, he rails against the destruction of cadavers through incision, disassembling, dissection, any type of destructive technical analysis. No one knows, he argues again and again, whether we can bring bodies back to life, now or much later, no one knows if we are alive now or if we only become truly alive after we die. Maybe bodies will return to life, but in a different way, not as bodies, not carnal, maybe there is a seed that appears in the body while it is alive, and it needs the unravished compost of the cadaver in order to grow, it needs the love of those who remain among the living to flower and accomplish its task—the savant explained. If we cut the germinating seed during dissection, or if we destroy it during cremation, the new being within us will not grow after our death. We should be more careful, more prudent with that which we cannot see and know nothing about, with our beings, which are much more complicated than they seem, created from multiple superimposed layers and from ever more refined bodies, we should verify our rushed scientific theories and our overbroad hypotheses, we should wait before we pronounce our skeptical and so-called realistic verdicts. We should try all known and unknown means to grow after death, after the passage, because there awaits a great mystery—explained the old savant in a learned and eloquent fashion.

I let myself be convinced by his arguments, deep within I agree with him fervently. Then I find myself led by the old scholar through a narrow maze in a basement of twisting hallways, with hidden niches and dark rooms. In one room, slightly better lit than the others, the old savant shows me, with pride and infinite love, as living proof of what he has said, a young man lying on a bed. The young man is dressed in a bizarre vestment, long, baggy, and out-of-date, made from a fabric of intense azure, an almost transparent fabric stitched with fine gold thread. The young man is on his side, facing the wall. When he turns slowly toward us, his lovely face shining with hidden light, I recognize Radu's features, as I knew them long ago, in that camp. The gangly but attractive teenager, with blue eyes and black curls, a skinny, honest teenager, but already worn down by the illnesses of pride and vanity, from girls' fascination with him.

In this hidden room in the basement, Radu seems to be in a strange state. As beautiful as a romantic genius, I think as I look at him, and my heart feels a sudden pain. He is lilac and translucent, he looks as fragile and as precious as a glass vase, from mysterious Etruscan graves. His eyes are wide and shining, as though burning with something difficult to name, with a fire flickering within. He is alive but looks like a specter, an odd and unsteady embodiment, destined to disappear, to die. Yes, that was it, he looks as though he has been brought back from the dead, he is delicate, diseased, quickless; he stares at me silently, with his turquoise eyes, crystalline and feverish.

I understand then that Radu has been saved from nothingness, brought back to life through magic, through

a demonic miracle, and that his life flows inside this enclo-
sure, like sand in an hourglass, inside the eternal prospect
of death, in its imminent contact. Radu lives there, on the
bed in the underground cell, like a body that cannot survive except in bed, protected, too delicate for the terrible
reality outside. Maintained by a secret, emotional energy.
Like a colorful cave creature, a blind, translucid protozoa,
but also a superior being, half angel and half demon, fed
a special liquid, a certain quick and dead water, cold and
warm, dribbled onto his lips with a pipette—mercury, I
believe. Radu is there on the bed, hidden and watched
over, because (I understand, both pained and fascinated)
a being like him cannot survive in the brutal air of raw
external light. My world, as I am given to understand
through a thought. But I, I can help him live through a
permanent transfusion of blood and love. Which I give.

I do not know how long the transfusion took. I
imagine, from the bitter taste in my mouth when I
awoke, that the ardor of that encounter under the earth
was one-sided. The underground creature could not
love. It could not anymore. In fact, I understood much
later, it does not matter, it is unimportant. Radu is the
small sun in the cave, he is my inner brother, he is my
sacred relic. He is a part of me. I will contain him forever, he exists inside, in eternity. He is my blue precious
stone, hidden in my chest. From time to time I take it

out, especially during those painful days of each month when I lose blood and live through my strange psychic states, when I am somewhat expanded: then I look at it, I contemplate it, with a kind of fascination. A strange fluid envelops me, is transmitted to me. I feel full again, whole, as though I wrapped my mind around myself, as though I opened, dartingly, the door of an apartment in my being, with living rooms and bedrooms and closets that I have not seen for a long time or that I have not yet known, as though I let a little air and a little light into parts of my being that I tend to neglect, to not frequent, to not give any credence, and which I would probably, little by little, forget, lose, annihilate.

When I look, from time to time, at my reflection in my precious stone, it vibrates. This vibration feeds me, brings me back to life. So I can endure, patiently, the rest of my long, ragged days, after falling from Reality into reality.

GUINEA PIG

Darling, in this life, just what are we meant to discover? What are we supposed to find? Why do I always feel like I have to solve some enigma, some riddle? And what is this enigma? And why am I always afraid I will lose the great wager, that I will stumble during a life-and-death obstacle course, that I will misinterpret a story, a code, a charade—given to me when and by whom and for what reason and to what end exactly?

For the past few years, I've become obsessed by the suspicion that I have forgotten something important, that I've overlooked something essential, something of absolute importance in this life—but what? Walking down a street with you, I saw a woman in the crowd, she was tall, beautiful, haughty; and suddenly the thought flashed through my mind that I had been there before, somehow, on the same street, with you, in the same crowd, seeing that tall woman, who seemed one of a god-chosen people, who had arrived to tell me something, something I did not understand. I stopped and looked around us—perhaps you don't remember little moments like these. I asked myself over and over: what have I not truly seen, what am I supposed to understand? What have I forgotten? When have I been here before? And what is with these gods, these priestesses, these superior women? Why do I have the nagging suspicion that I am repeating the same story over and over, the same script, in concentric circles, and that everything is pointless?

Another time, I went into the living room of our little apartment, repeating a line from Allen Ginsburg in my head, as a poetic mantra, something about a rose with a million petals, and I bumped into a vase, a large bouquet of brightly colorful flowers you had picked, and knocked it off the table. It fell, it shattered, and the flowers landed on the carpet in a strange pattern, circular, convoluted. I looked at the figure on the carpet and saw a giant, multicolored rose, hypnotic in the shock of its beauty, and I felt exhilarated. And out of the blue, I was struck, physically, on the back of my head by the simple idea, as clear as a verdict from someone outside myself, above myself, that I was still missing something important, although it was the nth time this seemingly unimportant event had happened, this strange coincidence, unexpected, between thought and objects and actions, between gestures and people and encounters, between poetry and dreams and ritual, seemingly foreign to each other but still connected by a subtle thread, coherently, by a logic my mind rejected. When I face this—how to put it—portal between the world and the mind that secretes a kind of tridimensional metaphor, we could say, because it is invisible and veiled, and it unfolds in space and time, and inside of which I live my life, I am always blind, always ignorant of the deeper meanings of these almost banal events, I always sleep through their simple and mysterious messages.

In fact, everything had become complicated, as puzzling as groping through a maze, but a strange maze, because it does not have right angles or perfect curves cut into thick hedges with little, brilliant leaves of deep green, as I had seen in churches or elegant parks, in pictures on the internet. This maze was quite domestic, it was my daily life, my real existence, so repetitive, so ordinary, with its rising, washing, eating, working, shopping, cooking, tidying, and sleeping, etc., but transformed into a hidden crossword puzzle, a kind of chess game with pieces larger than myself. I had to move carefully through the white and black squares, paying close attention, in order to notice the various characters and mysterious signs, tiny coincidences, unexpected synchronicities, in order to avoid the trapdoor squares that would shoot me dangerously back toward square one, or in order to jump ahead to the better squares, which will take me quickly toward the end. And when I thought I had learned something, that I knew something as clearly as I could, that I could use what little experience I had acquired up to then, suddenly the rules of the game seemed to change completely, I could not see the old characters, the landmarks were moved, the matches did not reoccur. I had to stop, I was lost, I tried desperately to use my power of movement, my first reasoning, my instinctive cunning, even the absurd hope that, whatever happened, everything would come clear, I would find a path, that I am not alone, that I have help—but for a time I am unable to make a move in this strange, three-dimensional chess game, I am blocked, I can do nothing but wait.

Next, I had the almost physical sensation that I was being watched, from above, from somewhere above where someone studied me, as though I were a white guinea pig with rose-colored paws, trapped inside an antiseptic universe built entirely from glass. A guinea pig who had to solve the equation to find the cube of sugar at the end of pathways that follow simple mathematical formulae, a process that would yield the intelligence quotient of the poor animal. The little guinea pig knows and does not know that it is being subjected to tests of its survival and evolution. In fact, it can tell something is going on, but it does not want to believe that this is real; instead, it wants to believe that it is favored by fate, privileged, from birth, to live in a closed world of antiseptic glass, where it is fed and cared for, with the aim of prolonging its life, even if it can tell that in the end it will be sacrificed. And even if it clearly understood that it was part of an important experiment, one that might forever change the destiny of its tame and mustachioed species, what use would this knowledge be? The result would still not depend on the guinea pig, however much intelligence it could put in play. It still would not be able to understand the technicians, who are much too high above, too far away, and who speak a language too complex, too sophisticated for its limited mental decoder and its archaic phonetic apparatus.

It has no other option than to hope and to pay close attention. Because it might lose not only its daily cube of sugar and tiny cup of water, but also its life, or what it thinks its life may be. It senses that the technicians do not wish it evil, maybe they are even generous, full of good intentions, and they try to help as much as they can, within the limits of the enormous distance between its world and theirs. They try to guide it with little marks, coincidences, symbols, so it can understand something beyond its banal existence, but what? What, exactly? To realize the rules of the game it has to play and the place in its mind where it happens? To change some of the rules in its favor, or to be capable of escaping the game entirely? To attempt to jump into another more complicated and more dangerous game, in its unknown mental circumvolutions? To transform into something else? Into another animal species? Or transanimal?

But into what, my God, into what? And I do not understand what exactly, although it seems that understanding is near, like a vibration, that it is right at hand, and it wraps around me, and it is immediately there. And what am I missing, mechanically, out of ignorance, in the present being of my present existence, like a machine on automatic pilot, like a lazy Pinocchio who will not turn into a real boy, like a ridiculous marionette who imagines it's alive and acts like a scared guinea pig, trapped inside a maze of antiseptic glass? And where in my life did I make a mistake, what was my error in my existence? What detail have I missed?

KORE

I am twenty-two years old. I am a student, I take the bus to the university every day, but the courses don't interest me too much. I don't sleep well, I have bizarre emotional flare-ups, where I think I know everyone on the street and that they ought to know me. Their faces all seem beautiful and familiar, I look them straight in the eyes and I suddenly want to embrace them, to love them. And it seems so strange to me, so painful it brings tears to my eyes, that they don't recognize me, don't see me, that I am a stranger to them and they never think to make any gesture of friendship. At night, I have relentless, haunting dreams, about sex, women, men, children, birth. Especially birth, birth, birth, birth. But whose, and how, in what manner, I can't tell, and for the moment I don't want to get married or to have children, not yet. Still, a child often appears to me in my sleep, a minuscule, white child like a long bean. This dream changes each time into a poem on the same subject, obsessive, filling entire notebooks. I don't really understand why these themes assail me, since I haven't started to do "it." I do have a classmate, Radu, a different Radu, who wants to go out with me, but I tell him no, he doesn't attract me, I don't like him.

Whenever we meet, I talk to Radu passionately about the difference between the soul and the spirit, about transcendence and sublimation, about deathlessness and reincarnation, and then I wander into other things, I recite poetry by Novalis and Hölderlin, I dance out my words with my arms and legs, making exaggerated, theatrical gestures; I wave intensely colorful silk scarves and wrap them around my face, seductively, as though I were onstage, auditioning for a romantic movie from another time, a bit out-of-date. I know that it's all silly and ridiculous, my private show for Radu, what I improvise from ideas I gather from the books I read voraciously, and sometimes, when I am improvising, I sense that I am playing a role that has existed for a long time, like an old type, very old, that has my name and that I fill for a moment with my young being. And in that dilated moment, I wonder for a second if "I am following the script," a script seems important, something that exists around me, but I do not know what the right text would be.

Radu watches me patiently, he listens, he tries to understand what it is I want. I talk to him about my soul, made up of multiple layers and wrapping and multiple levels, of which I only know one so far, the ground floor, but I imagine there are other floors above, rooms with fabulous treasures, as I have dreamed, several times, splendid palaces that grow above the top of my head. Or I talk to him about the pure and difficult loneliness to which I aspire, which would be enough for my proud and imaginary nobility, I perorate to him about my desire to live far from people, in the great and small absolute, in a wasteland or a convent in the mountains full of exquisite cells, I make speeches to him about destiny, choice, fate, and other pretentious things—silliness, stupidity, sweet eccentricities. When he walks me to the university bus stop, before I climb into the bus, Radu, exasperated, asks for the hundredth time what I am looking for, what I want from this world. I stubbornly give him the same response, I am looking for a coherent image of the world, one that will fit into my mind, one where I can find my place. Or maybe a coherent magic of the world. What could that be? Radu replies, he is interested only in palpable things, his engineering classes and me.

One day, in my third year, there was a terrible earthquake, 7.5 on the Richter scale, that shook the entire city. It was evening, around nine or so, and I suddenly heard a kind of moan from the depths of the earth, a long howl like a giant prehistoric animal, and all four walls of the room where I slept and read started to shake; a terrifying vibration shook the furniture and objects for several minutes. The books crashed down from the shelves, the desk and chair came to life, they creaked in their joints and slid over the wood floor, the ceiling lamp swung like a pendulum from one side to the other. The walls undulated like sheets of paper in the wind. As my bed jumped crazily up and down, I, frightened to the depths of every cell, paralyzed by a limitless terror, was sure that the end of the world and the last Judgment had come, to raise the dead from the earth and throw the living in Gehenna; then I thought that there had probably been a giant atomic explosion, somewhere faraway, and in the next moments of my life, it would destroy my world and the entire planet. Everything around me trembled menacingly and made a vast howl, a deep moan. A much more powerful energy shook everything and me as well, buried in my bed. The wave of giant and unbearable vibrations wanted to destroy everything. It was the end, the terminus, my death and the world's, I was sure of it. I had no other thought, I was liquefied with fear, I waited in terror to die. Nothing could follow such a shaking of the world, the demonstration of its frightening fragility. But, after two minutes, so long, so devastating, that terrible groaning from the depths of the earth became less intense, dissipated, the destructive vibration moved slowly away, like an invisible tide retreating, the furniture slowly stopped its strange motion, as though it had finally pulled its plug out of an unknown outlet, where it received, without wanting to, a high-voltage electric shock.

In the days that followed this long and powerful earthquake, which destroyed a quarter of the city and killed thousands of people, I was thrown into an awful panic. Because I realized for the first time how vulnerable I was in my young and, until then, immortal body, my street, my city of stone, concrete, and steel, my city full of tall buildings and boulevards, I realized with my entire being, with all my organs, just how flimsy the world is. I had thought my world, like a round, transparent ball of glass, was more powerful than destruction, shattering, death, when in fact it takes nothing more than a tremble of the earth's skin, the vomit of a volcano or the fury of a tsunami, not that much in the end, nothing at all, and everything goes down the drain. The human world ends. Suddenly I understood, with all my young flesh, that death is a powerful, palpable, and proximate reality. Death is. I saw its constant *presence* that stalked us from some high spot above, sometimes from a corner of the ceiling. For the first time, I perceived death with the body, its senses suddenly exceptionally sensitive, I intuited its strange entity, an entity of a certain real consistency, not like a precious and complicated abstraction that can be held at a distance with words and sophisticated analyses, the kind of thing I read in books of philosophy. I perceived it as a type of compact, self-enclosed energy, vibrating, lucid, set in an invisible but well-defined place in the space around it, and which may in some circumstances be felt outside the body, almost caressed with the senses.

I do not know whether it was then, in the days after the earthquake, when I volunteered from morning to night to help remove the wounded, or more often the bodies, from the rubble, that I encountered my own death. I don't think so, I felt more that it was death itself, death like our true destination, a total and omnipresent presence, a dark and all-powerful divinity, like a dense, impenetrable cloud over all our heads that was showing itself in all its intractable splendor. A powerful and hypnotic presence, driving us from behind like blind, powerless dolls, throwing us like sacks of grain into the enormous mouth made of millstones, of chaos, pulling us magnetically like heaps of iron filings, spread over the surface of the earth, because day after day I saw everyone on the street, including me, as dead people, as cadavers. Vertical cadavers, nervous and talkative. Cadavers of young men and young women kissing hungrily in the parks. Hundreds of grown cadavers seated rigidly in meeting halls or theaters. Sleepwalking cadavers, ambulatory specters, ridiculously assuming all kinds of tasks, trying desperately to seem alive, to forget. Important, official cadavers. Painted, gussied cadavers.

Little cadavers in curls in colorful strollers with pink and blue bow ties. Cadavers in my family, beside me, at dinner, in my house. And me, likewise, a cadaver. A young cadaver that believed it was, without a doubt, alive.

This overwhelming sensation filled me with a deep anger, with poison. A black water flowed through my nerves and my flesh, a dark shadow wrapped around me, within and without. Mute and almost disfigured with terror, I suffered because it seemed only I had been chosen to understand, with godlike omnipresence. It seemed like a bad omen had struck me in particular from somewhere on high, above people's heads, where, whether someone felt it or not, death, the authoritarian master of our world, was watching, was waiting. As though the one who felt it had been touched, irrevocably, by its pitiless breath. As though once you felt it in this way, physically, sensorially, you accepted it, you received it into your flesh, into your living and palpable cells, and you became truly mortal.

I felt it around me, I saw its evil shadow over many faces, I was haunted at the same time by the thought that the great and probably inevitable error, like an immemorial and irrevocable sin, is to let ourselves feel its presence physically, organically, to take it into our thoughts, no, into our souls, as though it were an absolute limit, with nothing afterward, and with no escape, when it is a passage, a transformation. Only from that fateful decision does it, death, become powerful, does it enter us through that tiny gate this thought leaves open in our cells, this strangely lucid thought, this sick consciousness, evil and cold like a mouthful of mercury. If I did not think of and accept death as the total end, as nothingness, within a point low in my abdomen and then in my solar plexus, and then in my mind, perhaps I would be saved from the taste of its metal patina, perhaps I would survive its cold breath and transform it, perhaps I would not die. The deep anger that flooded me was a death sentence, because I knew with an utter, shuddering certainty that I had allowed myself to be caught in this trap, as vulgar, as handy, as everyday as it is. But *it* is above, around the upper left corner of any place I might be, like a misty, tiny cloud, like an unseen but noticeable being with another type of sense; it sits there, watching me, wrapping around me from time to time with its shining, steady gaze, sending me mysterious signals, surprising coincidences, waiting patiently and inescapably. That is when I experienced Desolation.

During this period, I dreamed repeatedly about the end of the world, the apocalypse. I know, darling, lots of young people dream about catastrophes, perhaps they are scared of life, or they have the profound desire to save a world that seems too degraded, too rotten, or suffers too many earthquakes. In one of these dreams, a mysterious, secret cause made the entire earth barren, without any form of life aside from me and a young man. Together with him, *him*, one I do not know but feel close to, we must remake the human species—but better, wiser, nobler. The enormity of this mission frightens me, yet I also feel a certain fervor, I wonder in the dream whether I will be able to remember even the most elementary facts about the lost world, to teach humanity's first children—and it seems the only things I am sure I know are arithmetic, poetry, and music. Other times, I dream of the enormous, smoking ruins of a metropolis destroyed by a chain of atomic accidents, where I run desperately, in bare feet, through the total disorder, through the chaos around me, searching for an exit from this hell of rubble and cadavers. And, in my hurry, I drop the child in my arms, *my daughter*, a little creature who clings to my chest; in fact she is a plastic doll that looks something like me, and seems to live and not live at the same time, that seems to sleep. I run in every direction, I look for my daughter everywhere, with desperation and tears, to the other end of the world. And I cannot find her.

In another dream, everyone and everything, big cities and small, forests and mountains and fields, endless herds of animals and countless people all swirl downward, as though into a single, giant flood, into the mouth of a grand, dark abyss. Everyone and everything flow head-first into a frightening disorder, into a chaotic waterfall, livid with color, a mixture of all the colors of beings and things thrown into the rapids, a purple-gray color, deathly and terrifying. And I, in the middle of this flood of people drowning in the abyss, I fall as they do, headfirst, like a broken doll, through the enormous, dirty waterfall, I fall and I fall, with the fear of death in my soul, trying to escape from the tight carcass of my body caught in the torrent, writhing to pull off my body, this sea-diver's suit that entraps me, a hermetic box, a prison, and I cannot. Yet somehow, with a thought that comes from someplace else, from above, I know that if I want to save myself, I have to hold tightly to *his* hand, an unknown *him*, enigmatic, whom I cannot see but I feel close by, an intense presence, like a more powerful and wiser consciousness than my own. And in the end, as though by a miracle, in the last moment I save myself from the enormous diluvian current, and I reach a quiet field . . .

I float without a body, like a pure gaze, like an all-seeing presence, I float over a black, freshly plowed field, lined with hawthorn bushes full of bloodred berries, along the edge of a forest with leafless beech trees. It is autumn, a sunlit day, clear but not very warm, there is a sweet, relaxed sadness in the air. I float and I tell myself that in spite of the autumnal beauty I see about me and which wraps itself around me and exhilarates me, I will die, I will die, I will die, but this is nothing, this is nothing, I will keep dreaming, keep floating among the images and visions I have acquired over the course of my existence, just as I am floating now over the field. I will enjoy my memory, full of special moments I accumulated in life, I will consume them, and in this way fill up my eternity. But in my left ear, a strange voice whispers insidiously, "How will you access your dreams, the way you do now, if your brain dies along with the rest of your body? Only the brain can remember and dream. If it rots, you will not be able to enter the world of your memories and dreams. It will be an absolute, total darkness. It will be nothing but nothing." The voice is cold, the whisper is apodictic, the words sound maximal and final. In that moment, I forget the strange, elevated states that seemed to come not from my brain but from another part of reality, one vaster and less knowable, I forget the luxurious visions, preserved not in my brain but by a mysterious wavelength exterior to my neurons, I forget those powerful, vivid images, impregnated somewhere, in an invisible field, by a certain vibration, one higher and unexplored. In that moment, I forget the vibrant visions, I forget my timeless memory that connects with a certain, how to say it, *kingdom of images*. I forget everything—and an immense sadness drowns me and wakes me up.

•

In the dark days that followed the earthquake, it seemed to me that nothing mattered in this vulnerable world. Not me, not anyone else, not my philosophy classes or any "coherent image of the world." I felt a need to do myself harm, to lose myself. I wanted to destroy myself, as a punishment. I wanted to suffer intensely and to awaken, to be like other people and to awaken finally to reality. And one evening, I did. I did "it." I said yes to Radu just as I would have done to any other man, because it seemed to me there was no hope, no salvation, no escape from this enclosed but fragile world. One afternoon I went to Radu, pure and simple, and asked him to make love to me. He took a long look, with a joyful light in his eyes, mixed strangely with a wince, and he tamely subjected himself as though to an order he could not challenge, a categorical obligation. "It" was executed gently, affectionately enough, with a certain tender pity in his calm, skilled motions. It did not hurt much, in spite of my dramatic, terrible imagination. At the end, I saw three drops of blood on the sheet and fell exhausted into sleep.

I am walking, holding Radu's hand, toward a lonely church, in a rough, barren field. I wear white, my hair decorated with pink and white ribbons fluttering along beside me in the soft wind, coming from who knows where. When we reach the church, at the vestibule entry, Radu takes me in his arms and carries me over the threshold, as is correct. Inside, the church is clean and empty, a gold slant of light, an ancient and clean light enters through the tall, narrow, glassless windows. We approach an archaic stone table, a kind of altar, in front of the iconostasis. We each have a large, white candle in our hands, both are lit. Now we must officiate, together, a mass about something we do not know, we do not know, and for which we are not prepared. I tell Radu that he will have to be the priest, and I will be the assistant who accompanies him. When we begin to chant, stumbling over the words, we notice that melodious phrases in an unknown language begin to flow mysteriously from our mouths, and they fill the church with a divine, wondrous harmony. There is a pleasant scent in the air, aromatic substances seem to burn in a far-off corner. The church slowly fills with a brilliance, ever more intense, blinding . . .

I woke from this dream in tears, and for one intense moment, I hated Radu, furiously. But he was not to blame.

MOON

I left Radu late that fateful evening. When I arrived home,
I dove into my bed and, feeling strange, almost like I was
drunk on wine, dizzy with a heavy, sedating vibration, I
tried to understand what had happened to me. And all I
could put together was that I was foreign to myself, and
that I did not know me or love me, that I was far from my
real self. A self that had just begun to emerge and that
announced its presence only through dreams and bizarre
states that were impossible to understand. I was seized by
an immeasurable desperation, and for reasons I cannot
explain, I picked up a round mirror from the bed table, and
I put it between my slightly separated legs. I wanted to see,
to *see myself* in all my ignorance and disarray. And what I
saw amazed me, horrified me, and I fell into a kind of void.

I faced a massive, high gate, a monumental gate. It looked
like the imposing entrance of a temple, the top curves into
an arch, and it appeared to have been cut from a pinkish

mahogany, shot through with black, serpentine veins. When I touched it, the gate seemed to become warm marble. The two large doors of the gate, their surfaces rounded and dense, were slightly open, and through them I could see another set of gates, smaller, and the beginning of a dark hallway. I tried to pull them open, but they burned me, as though they were incandescently hot metal. I looked at them with fascination, the burn hurt, and a tremor seemed to enter me, with a kind of terror, a sacred horror. Then, someone on my left, maybe *him*, a man's voice, whispered to me to pass under the bottom edge, where the opening seemed larger. And so it was, I went in.

It was tight inside, dark and warm, and it seemed I was not alone, *he* took my hand. In fact, I seemed to take my hand, I held my own hand, I was the boy and the girl who began to go down the entryway. There was also a presence beside us, and the air was vibrating with tension, like the head of a drum. The presence, a kind of me but more adult, taller, said to me that this was my gate, my own, that I *must* pass through this trial. And then I was only the boy.

The girl took my hand and motioned I should be silent. In the room we entered, with gold decorations on the walls and heavy, red velvet curtains on the windows, there was only one large chair of brown, aged leather, a vanity with an oval mirror and many kinds of boxes, filled with jewelry and makeup, and, beside the table, a simple and narrow bed of lacquered wood, covered with tattered white fabric. *She* lay down naturally on the bed and motioned for me to come near. To lie next to her, on top of her. I didn't understand what she wanted.

The girl was attractive and about my age, wearing a lace dress of a luminous yellow-gold color, her hair was red, and her round face was covered in brown freckles. She stood up, came to me and embraced me gently, boyishly, then she pushed me onto the chair and silently rubbed a finger across my lips. And this time I was not afraid or disgusted or nauseous, like in the past, this creature different yet similar to me, beautiful and still repulsive, who used to engender an irrepressible impulse to reject her. I sat in the chair, watching as she arranged her hair, her clothes, and I felt something changing inside me, growing, fattening in the lower part of my abdomen. Then she stood and went toward the bed again, pointing to something in the front of my white pants. I looked down, horrified and amazed.

And suddenly, I heard noises outside, cries and complaints and curses, and a diffuse threat caused imperial gates to vibrate like a drum. The room changed into a kind of church. On the white marble of the altar, in front of the closed imperial gates of the iconostasis, she was lying faceup, her arms alongside her body, and she whispered fervently for me to lie on top of her, to lie down, to take her. I did not understand. I looked at her amazed, frightened, and deeply ashamed, even disgusted. A new fear began to overtake me, a sharp sound whistled in my ears. I grew slightly nauseous and frightened again. A powerful attraction, almost tangible, magnetic, pulled me forcefully toward the altar.

Then the altar became a boat. I tried to resist. A kind of moaning, a kind of vibration threatened me from outside, it was the cries and complaints and curses, and she whispered to me hurriedly, fervently, pleadingly, almost imploring, to get into the boat, to flee with her. To *pass over* finally. And I got in. I did not imagine it could have been so difficult, so tiring. So abrupt. It was as though I had to jump over a wide, dark ditch full of deep water. As though I had to scale a wall of water-worn rock, or to climb a steep, slippery hill.

She was on the prow, her white-gold dress flowing in the wind, and she waved to me. She looked small and luminous, faraway, like a far-off mountain, a phantom, a pagan goddess. Then I was there too, on the prow, I do not know how I got there, but there she was below me, I could feel her body trembling, I moved slowly up and down with her, following her breathing, as though

I were on a light, wooden raft, rocking on currents of warm liquid. Now we were on a dark, choppy sea. I felt the giant depths of water below me. We floated like a scrap of wood, the dark waves crashing around us. I wanted to sleep.

I wanted to stop knowing. But she shook me more powerfully and whispered in my hear that I had to enter inside, to penetrate. I did not understand. I was amazed, horrified. Her calm face was very close to mine and yet it seemed faraway, as though shining with a lunar light from somewhere high, over the mountains.

Her round and luminous face, full of little brown freckles. Something began knocking against my body again, that strange vibration invaded me intensely, as though an unexpected electric shock went through my muscles and bones. I was cold with a kind of fear, it was dark, and among the snowdrifts she looked luminous and faraway again, she waved to me. She emitted a tiny flame, as though from a cigarette lighter, along a thin mark suspended in the air like a phosphorescent cord, coming toward me, approaching, threatening my chest, to ignite my body, to burn me.

And then I penetrated. I entered.

I felt her beneath me, she was soft and warm. The fire burned somewhere near my body, it was a kind of coal that slowly consumed my feet, then my thighs, then my abdomen. It was suffocating, like being beside a burning forest. I wanted to flee, to hide, but then something like a burning wave, like an electric current began to climb over me.

I had not imagined it could be so difficult, so sudden. As though I had to pass through gates of old mahogany, to open complicated, rusted padlocks. It was hard to make room, I tired quickly. On a red granite mountain there was a narrow valley, barely lit by the moon. I had to pass between cave walls that scratched my shoulders, then down a narrow, rickety bridge suspended over a great height. Below, dark water flowed. I heard her crying softly, sighing. She waved to me delicately.

In the valley I came upon a thick, humid forest. Eyes glowed in the darkness, there was rustling, fluttering, sharp birdcalls. It was difficult to make progress, I pressed my body forward, feeling with my hands. It seemed that there were all kinds of beasts around me, watching me, and at a certain moment I heard a horrifying and enigmatic howl.

Then I began to descend. I felt her next to me, soft and warm, I felt her around me, in a cascade of laughter. The waterfall flowed into a cave, its echo made the walls vibrate. I descended a steep stairway of warm, slippery rock. And at the bottom, below, warm, warm, red, red, then darkness. The fire had reached my chest, it was a kind of sweetly burning coal that had already turned the rest of my body to ash.

I walked frightened down the steps, rather I slid, there was a kind of suction, a magnetic force that pulled me into the vertiginous depths. I heard cries, laughter, whispered encouragements, and vague chords of music. I saw flashes above me and comets shining in the heavens, whizzing past me, disappearing vertiginously below. There was a strange smell of earth and ether, of rot and holy oil. The strange vibration came over me again, but more powerfully, it shook me until I thought my form would break, or whatever remained of my body. The burning coal reached my heart, I saw nothing but red, everything looked purple and aflame, everything was burning brightly. Then my sight went completely dark. And I felt I would be scattered in all directions, that I would die, that I would disappear, transformed into pure darkness. Something had left me. Something hot had gone out of me. An arrow of fire, a small, translucent and living sphere, a liquid stream of meteors and planets. For a moment I was no more, or I was the entire world. A vast space, a beatitude. An immense and loving darkness. Then I fell back into the boat, onto the raft, into my body. I felt something near me. Someone was beside me.

We were in a round and intimate hall, like a tiny grotto. A diffuse luminescence inexplicably revealed a domed, low ceiling, made of pinkish granite scraped smooth as marble. *She* held my hand, she smiled at me. She was wearing the same lace dress of luminous colors, now gold. She was just as beautiful and mysterious as when she took my hand the first time. But she seemed much larger. Her smile reminded me of my mother.

In the middle of the round hall I saw a throne. It was a double throne of gilded wood, whose high back showed carved lettering. A narrow red carpet led from our feet to the throne. I walked down the warm and velvety carpet, and she walked with me. She pressed against my left side, so close, as though she were walking with my left leg, and I felt an odd intuition pass through me.

We arrived at the throne. The golden throne made itself into a table. It was a long wooden table, covered with a pure white cloth, like an immaculate sheet. And on the table was a wooden box. A long, black box, in which something was lying down, someone. Hand in hand, smiling, we leaned over to see what was inside. And what we saw reconciled us, it gave us joy.

In that moment, the cries and complaints fell quiet, the drum stopped vibrating. I opened my eyes. I was in my bed again, with the small mirror next to my left thigh, I was curled up and shivering beneath the sheet. It was long past midnight. And from my bed, I saw, though the window—with its round, gold face, full of little brown dots and dark craters, like the face of a pregnant woman—the appearance of the enormous, majestic, perfectly full moon.

OH, DARLING

Oh, darling, what do you know, so fed up with love, so tired,
exhausted by love, you tell me about the sufferings of your mental
circumvolutions, about your complicated abstract, logical issues
with morals and sex. You are as empty as a crumpled paper bag,
as a broken vial, you are disgusted that you have fallen into the
carnal trap again, you are sick that you let your fecund liquor
escape your body again, your precious, sacred, virile fire. But
what do you know about me, about the soft, disheveled duvet
under which you lost yourself for a second, you wanted to escape
your unhappy, stubborn mind for a flashing moment; did you
go out, into the ocean, into the void, to the boundless, the free?
What do you know about women? You don't know anything,
you have no clue, although you think you know everything.

For you, the body is not that important, it is a simple tool,
a kind of knife, an uncomplicated weapon, it is an appendix
you use to excite your mind. To believe you possess something,
another being, reality, power. For me, the body is almost every-
thing. You men, you are born almost completely made, your

packaging is more or less the same from start to finish, while we women, we keep changing, like insect pupae, like butterflies, like the seasons and planets; periodically something happens to us, our bodies will not leave us alone, we cannot forget we exist while they enclose us. This body is a suffering that I for one don't understand, it is an enigma whose key has been lost, it is a mystery I don't know what to do with. Your understanding, darling, is on the level of calculations, rationalizations, mental projections— my understanding happens through the body, through flesh and blood, through a strange assemblage of sensations-emotions-perceptions, closer or farther away, and sometimes even through sur-perceptions.

You are always afraid to come too close to physical pain, to the miseries of the body, to physical degradation and death. You approach these topics with endless caution, with horror, and you wrap them in all types of fictive cocoons. While I cannot make abstractions out of my humors, blood, uterus, ovaries, out of the cyclic destruction, the cyclic resuscitation, and the repeated possibility of growing a living seed in the depths of my body, because there something unclear, something mysterious is hidden, like life on this planet, like eternity in this universe, something that cannot be otherwise received and grown and understood. It is a kind of delicate and slow awakening that comes along with repeated bodily changes, as inexorable as the seasons, years, eons, it is a kind of stumbling initiation, chaotic, in which you come to intuit the fact that your body is repeating who knows what planetary law, cosmic cycle, or sur-human ritual. Time brings an initiation, without a special school and without a master, or with teachers of happenstance, who may be people or things or events. An initiation we withstand through our flesh and our inner torments, endured in a dream or awake, in who knows what room, on an ordinary bed, in a train, on the seashore, in an elevator, on the roof of an apartment building, sometime, somewhere, at random. An initiation into primitive, odd mysteries, whose meanings were lost long ago or were never completely known, and as wordless, muttering guides we have only the body and instinct and patience, and our many interior images.

On this odd road, imposed by itself, my only guide and only compass is my being, trapped inside this sexualized and dreaming fleshly uniform, which I have to observe with close attention. My being is a mystery and a tool at the same time, it is the investigator and the test subject, with it I have to manage and with it I must pay for my progress. But the progress is slow and roundabout, as I have told you, because it is full of forgetting and confusing signs, broken by long pauses and backsliding, because the signs are not clear enough, the trails not obvious enough, the meanings are ungraspable but seem insignificant, like rebuses with pulsating images, fascinating and ever changing. Oh, darling, you ask ironically for the name of my first guide, my first teacher. You imagine it was a man. Know now that I initiated myself alone.

LOVE STORIES

There were once an emperor and an empress. They lived in a tiny grotto and were brother and sister. The grotto was in your heart. Flesh. Just flesh? The emperor and empress longed in vain for a total, genetic fusion, from which a child should result. Their sensual embraces produced nothing but high-pitched sounds and sparks, with no product. Their physical love gave them nothing but images, dreams, visions.

One afternoon, when they had lost all hope, a child as small as a bit of crystal appeared in them, or better put, in between them. What was it like? It was transparent and fragile, like a small, white bean, and its minuscule cradle was the heart shared between the emperor and empress. Its minuscule cradle was flesh. Just flesh? Inside their heart were you. You! How, exactly? I do not know. I do not know. I do not know anymore.

Child, are you sleeping, are you sleeping? Rock me,

save me! Child, don't go to sleep! Don't fall! Don't die! Wake up, wake me up! Rise from my heart.

I step into the world. Into unctuous material. Into warm perplexity. It is really my body, it is really the world! A kind of grenade with the pin removed. A burst pomegranate, overripe. Its core is pink and juicy, full of round, dark-colored seeds, glowing gently, waiting to explode. The core unfolds slowly, like the immense bud of an unknown flower, in my heart blinded by sunlight.

Slowly, world, do I enter you. You swallow me, I swallow you. You devour me, I devour you. The voluptuousness of disappearance. Slowly do you possess me, consume me, disintegrate me. Slowly I take possession of you, digest you, metamorphose you. Drops of fecund sweat hang soft from the leaves. Pieces of burning quartz scintillate in the mountains high and deep. Frothing rivers crash onto elastic shores of flesh. I wait. I wait for you.

Taste the oyster, taste the oyster! Oh la la! Oh la la! Soft and pale is the taste of the pampered jellyfish. It bites, it bites lips, pomegranates, breasts, pineapples. It sucks, swallows, there are oysters open on the shore. Go into the warm water, let yourself drown slowly. You taste me, I distaste you. You swallow me lazily, I swallow you hungrily. Your knife sticks in the waves. I am froth melted ashore. Oh la la! Oh la la!

He walks naked through the house, he moves untroubled like the perfect beast, innocent of its own nakedness. He moves the long muscles of his thighs, agile and unabashed like a wild man, or the first human, there, in the virginal forest, where only we two live, alone, alone. I look at the soft, delicate knot hanging between his thighs. I am amazed every time I see this contorted root of a woody plant; its spasmodic beginning has gone outside to explode into the leaves and florescence somewhere within.

There is something beautiful and horrible in it. Something so softly organic and yet absurd, aberrant, like an unhappy invention of someone who did not know how to finish the lower part of the abdomen. It looks added-on—a bunch of grapes, a velvet sack or a perfidious grenade—it looks like it was stuck on afterward, made up of corporeal leftovers.

The soft and silky knot surprises me every time I see it. The sight surprises, perplexes, and fascinates me; I try to understand. My imagination is blocked by a kind of gently frightened amazement. As happens each time I see something that is like this world: beautiful and horrible at the same time, animal and holy, a body member and an instrument of visionary exhilaration, that understands in the end this fact: what is both created and creative is just as much a hunk of meat as it is an enigma, an escape, *a path*.

Nickel faucet, living fringe with spasmodic knots, corydalis root, flaming sword, bell-headed snake, burnt-smelling sack, bumpy nose, god's trombone, spotted egg with leaping walnuts, tom thumb, spiny fig, softly dangerous bangle, Rappaport, hanging bells, tassel, flipper, sweet tuber, smithy's hammer, planter, cosmic plunge. Oh la la! Oh la la!

The yellow angel man enters the red angel woman. A spark of golden azure! A frothy light, a starry lace! He fills her silken palace with ardent dynamite and finishes deep within. Following the burning red thread, he makes his way slowly, he descends gently toward the center. He makes way, makes way, makes way, and he deposits himself in the sanctuary. A droplet.

She waits for him there, behind the small gold door covered with purple dampness. Ah, pink and bruised,

dew-covered purple! Ah, velvet fire, sweet abyss, undulating sea of soft furs, overwhelming avalanche of cotton
candy, crepe fountain to the other world, flesh heaven of
the deep.

He knocks slowly, slowly, harder, harder. He forgets
the way back, the way ahead. He knocks, still knocks.
Knocks and knocks and knocks. No one and nothing
answers. He knocks, he hits. And he forgets, forgets why,
how, because, forgets everything. He loses himself. He is
surrounded by a maternal, magnetic, overwhelming darkness. He only feels a widespread heat. A fire. Dissolving.
Disaster. And he gives up his spirit at the threshold.

Only then does the blue angel woman open her deli-
cious palace and deliciously explode. What rainbow, what
flowering vibrations, what spouting fountains! A spark of
azure, a frothy light, and starry lace! The angel woman
enters the angel man. Into the green empire enters the
pink empress. To drink his droplet. Gold. Salvation.

You are my instrument, you are my tool, you were born
for me. For me were you thought, were you shaped. Your
body was conceived for my body in particular, there in
the depths, in the small cell, double, triple, quadruple,
where that which was taken, was reft from me, was tra-
versed by a deep valley, in you was united, added to, and

pulled into a machine of war. You were created for me, you know it now, you see it when you sprout leaves, you flower in me like a waterfall, like an explosion, like long ago, in the narrow cell, in the pearly sphere, in beatitude.

I am in you, I am there, I lose myself, I will die, I am afraid to disappear, and I do disappear into nothingness for a moment, when a small sphere of fire leaves me—a fall, a cliff, my life goes toward you, a round, burning breath, and after there is only ash, nausea, the evil of a painful lack where the sweet-horrible memory remains of a falling-rising.

I am your instrument, I am the exotic fruit of your teeth, I am the food for your insane appetites, I am the drug that makes you die and rise again, the gravestone that crushes and makes you eternal, I am the chisel that sculpts you from within, in a star-filled cavern, I am your fated instrument, I am made for you.

I want to annihilate you, to destroy you, to be you, for us to be one. You want to annihilate me, to destroy me, to be me. I was born for this, I am your instrument, we will be, finally, ONE!

They stared at each other, fascinated, for a long time. As though their naked bodies, on the bed with white sheets, were two enormous, stupefied diamonds. He saw, in the black iris of her eyes, his true face for the first time. Illuminated with yellow-blue rays. Solar. She encountered herself for the first time, the small sacrificed goddess, forgotten of herself, in the haloed outline in the blue iris of his eyes.

Their naked bodies stared at each other, unmoving, they sucked each other in through their eyes, furiously, as though caught within an invisible vacuum, as though they might finally fall into each other, their shapes mixed at the halfway point, like two reflections in a stripe of sunshine, captured in a round mirror—and then they might disappear, evaporate, to be finally one. Between them, nothing but a short burst of lightning.

When the older sister opened the door, at first she saw only two large pools of light on the bed. When the older sister opened the door, for a second she saw naked twins, touching and looking at each other through the thin, gilded frame of a transparent mirror. And she recognized, in the large, white bed, the vision she had searched for, for a lifetime.

To undress you, to wash you, to dry your body with a rough cloth, to kiss it from the veins of the neck to the soles of the feet. To touch, shaking with a kind of holy terror, the delicate skin under the soft sheet. To fall on my knees, to fall from your feet. You do not know how much purity lies in this act. In my mind, I already see a thick field of tall corn, glimmering in the summer light, and I laugh as I walk through; the wide, rough leaves scratch me, they leave red lines on my arms, the succulence of their stalks exhilarates me, I want to taste them, to bite them, to chew them. You are the scented palm tree blooming between the banks of an opulent, green oasis, which appeared out of the blue in the field; farther on, I see a soft mountain coming rapidly toward me and that will slowly crush me; I see, I see, you are a double waterfall, both hot and cold, that drowns and revives me in a flash.

I am far now, I am a believer in India or Bengal, I face the altar, I kiss the cold blue lingam, I offer yellow saffron flowers and colorful sweets in its lap, I paint my lips purple, I am ready to prostrate myself, to rend myself before your godlike feet, to immolate myself voluptuously in the temple of your body.

I caress your bare body below the soft sheet. I tear the white sheet with my teeth. I see you rise in all your splendor, your cob of corn, firm waterfall, thin tree that crucifies and savagely flowers within me. Your small, burning flowers explode through me into the world. To be me no more. To be only shining sweat on summer leaves.

You have no idea how much holiness runs through this void. How much limitlessness. How much sacred vibration unites me with the world. How much beatitude.

Lord, nothing is left of him but a residue: a child. It is my child, my longed-for child. Which I permitted. To come to light. To come back. To be one. He fills me, he sates me. The child sates his mother. Come into me, from me, go back, inside, you sate me, you destroy me, you complete me. My sacrifice is welcome. The altar smells of flowers and holy oil. Here was your place. Here is your end. The mother devours her child. The child sates the mother. The mother swallows the child. The child gives birth back to the mother. Oh la la! Oh la la!

The world, the whole world is a long, rich vestment. A female-male dress. I wove it for you, it is the work of my hands. Wear it, wear the rivers and aurora borealis, the cities, wastelands, and mountains. Vest yourself with forests and cloud towers and fields full of summer harvest. Vest yourself with the whole world. So we can rise again over the earth, in the shining light and divine breath, so we can be again ONE!

CODA

The little female lies lazily on the couch. Her body is thin, almost a diagram, the pink-purple color of sweet-rotting blackberries. She delectates a dark green crystal cup, down which run silver beads and sweat and pearls and champagne. White.

From the viscous, soft velvet of the cherry-red couch, her black curls fall in frothy rivulets onto the floor. Next to her sits a small golden lion who gazes, with its tongue hanging out, at her pointed, pink-purple tits and her negative sex, just visible between her thighs. They are silent.

Around the couch wild animals prance. An indigo dialectical snake pokes its menacing and lugubrious eye through the lace. A white lizard runs here and there, leaving an unstable trail of mercury. Small gold tigers gently tease each other, as suavely as royal swans, through the bookish air.

Oh, but the couch is suspended! High above the round, barren attic, of yellow clay and stone, on the peak of a maroon, perfectly conical mountain. It is surrounded by rivers, evil and maleficent. The wind's color is disturbed. From dark waters, small, desperate heads emerge, they are the systematic worshipers. They scream with red, wet mouths at the goddess. The green dogs bark. The indigo snake hisses. The tigers growl with jealousy squared.

Fine, but what is the small female doing? She lies lazily on the couch and rubs her fingernails. From time to time, she sips from the crystal cup shining green, silver, pearl, and clover. She glances upward. And what does she see?

She sees an anthracite-black sky, abstract, full of the severed heads of her former lovers and worshipers. In color, in a line, like in a text illuminated with birds, insects, plants, and other hieroglyphics.

Finally, what should all this mean? What is the woman doing there? Is she waiting? She is waiting. As always, she is waiting. For a year. For a century. For an eternity. Ever since the sexual division of the angelic and organic world. Ever since the removal of the positive from the negative sex. Since the splitting of the sphere with four legs. Since the lord began the universe. She is waiting. In the meantime, she drinks champagnes of words, holy vibrations, and archetypal images.

And he, a young man, almost a child, appears far

away, running, running, his body naked, skinny, pink-purple like the froth of a sweet-rotting blackberry, with his
dangling sex in bloom like an apple branch, running, running with the Olympic flame in his left hand, running
for an eternity, since he lost his droplet in the magnetic
abyss, running and creating with his flight this story and
the world.

Oh la la!
Oh la la!

INTERLUDE

You think, darling, that there is only one kind of love. You are sitting beside me, with your elbows on the table, in front of a glass of vodka, I see your skeptical smile, a bit tired, through your two or three days' stubble. You think it is just a physical thing between a man and a woman. An encounter between two vain skins and two egotistical brains who want to possess each other, devour each other, destroy, annihilate. This irresistible and un-understandable attraction, sweetly frightening, which you project irrepressibly onto the other, which promises you liberation. That unbearable tension of senses, hormones, cells, at times exhilarating, more often humiliating, that wants to discharge itself into the other.

Do you know how many things or beings may be loved the way we love people? You only have to expand your point of view a bit, to dilate the optical diaphragms of interior vision, to let a little more light into the dark room inside yourself. A little more warmth. Animal, meteorological, vegetable, planetary, astral. To leave the exposition a little longer, as always. To not move

*the goal for no reason. To sit, calm, to wait. And after a while,
you will observe strange formations and unexpected develop-
ments on the sensitive film of your meninges.*

*How the sky pours over the field of grass and impregnates
it with millions of tiny, scented flowers. How clouds gather and
rain over forests out of a pure erotic attraction, leaving their
countless tongue-wet nipples on the spicy peaks of beech trees,
oaks, and poplars. How from the most intense devotion, gnats
let themselves be burned by the light bulb or candle flame. How
trees grow straight toward the sky, from the seed hidden deep
in the earth, attracted by the most irresistible and loving call.
How from a tender idea of sacrifice, goats and gazelles finally
let themselves be caught and devoured by lions and panthers, as
a kind of ritual mating.*

*The way a young woman may love the hair at the bottom
of the tub, after the last bath her lover took before he left her. Or
the way a mature woman may love a pair of sneakers, new and
sweaty, only because she cannot dare to love the much younger
man in front of her. Or the way an old woman may discreetly,
tenderly encourage her man to grow closer to a younger woman
and to enjoy the spark that returns to his eyes. Or the way a
very old woman, forgotten by everyone, devotes herself to her
dogs and cats, mice and spiders, she loves her flowers in their
pots with a mystical devotion; then she goes to the church and
prays for us and for the world.*

I have many examples of these unusual loves, darling,

types not recorded in wise, dry books. But what do we really know about the way the sun loves as it casts its ardent light on the earth and keeps it alive, at the cost of its spectacular consumption? Or how the planets, comets, and meteors arrange themselves and move harmoniously around the sun, out of their pure devotional exhilaration? Or how all and all of it, suns and planets, hierarchies of visible beings and invisible powers, galaxies and abysses of particles of infinite parallel worlds, all and all of it creates us, feeds us, sends us waves of thought and energy, keeps us alive, sends us discreet and mysterious messages and reshapes us continuously, only through love, through pure, endless love. Because what is love but the supreme intelligence—fusional, alive, conscious—of the universe? If the universe is eternal and harmonious, then the universe is conscious; if the universe is conscious, then the universe means attraction, union, love, interpenetration. How could this world exist, how could it last without destroying itself, eroding itself, disappearing, if it were not encompassed moment by moment in an enormous torrent of love?

Darling, hear now that when you are not around, or anyone else, and in my aloneness I do not know what to do with my hands, with my yet unfulfilled, unfinished being, I want to caress everything I see, shiny doorknobs, worn-out rugs, half-open cabinets, and kitchen appliances—everything that you, at some point, have touched. Everything seems sensual to me and warm; when rubbed gently they awaken, they feel cared for, *they open their shining eyes and push forward wet, avid lips, trembling and alive they call me into a strange embrace. And I feel I can comprehend everything, absorb it through my skin, my eyes, my lips, drench myself enigmatically in you. I offer myself in joy to doors, rugs, small objects around the house; they now are a part of me. This is how I move inside, I kiss myself and I caress myself. An ancient mother awakens inside me, an enormous woman who calls constantly for her prey and her stomach wants to ingest and transform the entire world. This great world where you are often missing, where you let yourself dissolve like a handful of salt in a vast, transparent sea.*

But let me tell you about some other things that happened.

TWO WOMEN

Do you remember? A few years ago, we had some things to take care of in Constanţa. We climbed down from the crowded train in the morning, we walked through the heaps of luggage and groups of noisy kids on vacation who yelled insults and shouted at each other. We went through the tall, glass entryway of the station, almost empty at that hour, and we went to the street. In order to see the city a little, we decided to walk toward the center, avoiding the main street for some empty side streets. Cutting across a park, we found the earth was still damp, and a cool humidity, slightly salty, floated over it. Can you feel the sea? You asked and then bought me a small bouquet of white, spicy hyacinths.

Only that afternoon, killing time before the train left, did we go to the seaside. There were fairly few people there, older people mostly, walking up and down in the sharp and salty sea air. The cloudy morning had changed into a luminous day. On the top step of a concrete staircase leading down to the sea, we sat in dry grass, among some plastic glasses and torn paper left from the night before. Below, there was a happy group of kids running and shouting. They might be the same as from this morning, I thought. Only later, once we had calmed down from the agitation around us, trying to take in the vast and open atmosphere of the beach, did I see the women.

There was a couple below, at the other end of the concrete steps. Better put, there were two shadows holding each other, one taller woman with her arm around the smaller shadow. Like us, I thought. They were at the end of the stairs, two small shadows that looked so much like us; I felt close to them, fraternal, as though I were looking at us from outside. The immense sky, surprising for our city eyes used to thick, tall buildings, fell over us with its splendorous, giant towers of shining clouds, white and faraway. A kind of gentle liquefaction passed through me slowly. I watched the sea for a long time, there were tall, choppy waves, their churning white froth looked like the pure and precious saliva of a giant liquid mammal. Only later, when the taller of the shadows at the end of the stairs removed her arm from the other's shoulders, turning to show something, was I surprised.

It was a woman. In fact, there were two women. Two young women, leaning against each other, embracing. Without intending to I jumped, I tensed. Something, like a bit of electricity, vibrated in my chest. Was it perhaps these girls? I leaned closer to you, while you did not seem to have noticed anything special—it's good you exist, I surprised myself thinking, like a well-behaved woman. I tried to look just at the sea, its liquefaceous crashing, but I could not avoid glancing toward the two women.

The taller pointed something out on the horizon, a seagull, a wave, a boat, then she protectively put her arm back around the other's shoulders, trying to shield her from the cool breeze. They might be sisters, I thought, quickly ashamed of my judgmental imagination. An older sister maternally teaching the younger. Or maybe they were just friends, schoolmates, teenagers a little in love with each other, learning about love together, waiting for their first real boy. I looked at the sea again. There was so much agitation, such restlessness, it smelled rotten and wet, of algae and dead oysters, a sharp smell, aggravating.

Perhaps my eyes were tricking me, but no, there were two women. Young women. And no, they did not look like sisters or classmates; something sensual in the way the arm of the first woman held the smaller woman's shoulders, and gently caressed her along her spine, reminded me of something else, referenced something else. But what, where? And I bounced around inside myself, and I felt how tense I was. I wanted to pull close again to you, while you were watching the sea absently, I felt the heavy weight of your arm on my shoulders.

Then I suddenly and silently rebelled against my fears, I wondered whether I wouldn't be able, at the drop of a hat, to embrace, in this sensual way, another woman. A kind of vacuum struck my solar plexus, then a warmth. And after a long moment of fear, a salvo of colorful images rose from some deep part of me, a burst of an intensity I did not understand.

Yes, I had to answer myself, with a kind of shaking in my chest and arms. I saw it once in Cristina's eyes. My constant companion from high school was unchanged, after so much time, in my panoply of interior images. Her—we took long walks together in the afternoons, after school, through the twisting streets of our provincial town, arms around each other's waist. Her—we exchanged long, friendly and inflamed letters, even though we saw each other every day in the gray hallways of our girls' school. Her—in our long discussions, I would advance bold and noble abstractions, oh, how lofty, how abstract. I even wrote sonnets about her blue, Germanic eyes, eyes like rigid, transparent crystal, the opposite of my black, southern eyes. I even dedicated prose poems to her. She dedicated a knights-and-armor novel to me. Fire and inspiration flowed between our spirits, devotion and intensity. We dreamed at one moment of getting married, having identical wedding dresses and inviting the entire school to the wedding. Cristina, passionate and absolute in her words and gestures, left me unexpectedly for a tall boy, blond and pale. I ran into her only much later, completely by chance, a few years ago, on a street in the capital. I was darting across a busy intersection, in a large wave of people, when someone grabbed my hand and stopped me. At that moment I did not recognize her, I did not know who she was. I gaped at this strange woman in front of me, then bit by bit, a veil dropped from my eyes and I saw Cristina again. We gazed at each other silently, for a long moment. We gazed intensely, hungrily. Aside from two thin wrinkles around her mouth, and slightly lower cheeks, Cristina had the same blue crystal eyes, shadowed now by a hint of grief. I read in the ardor with which she gazed at me the same disturbed and thirsty recognition I felt for her. For a moment, a translucid, pearly sphere took shape around us and insulated us from the din of the street. The sphere was unchanging, it was, I do not know how, outside of space and time. Inside of it, our reunited gazes produced the same eternal electric discharge, the same quivering ravenousness. Then I asked her how things were. She had two kids now, a boring job, and a man who drank too much. We parted with a promise to meet again, but neither of us was convinced we would. And yet, we had once shared the same odd, today unintelligible, ecstatic joy.

And now? Not now, I told myself, remembering you, sitting nearby and looking silently at the sea, dragging on your cigarette, that story seemed naïve, puerile, banal, even though somewhere at home I still had Cristina's letters and my diary from that time, all well-hidden. A story from puberty, the chaos of physiology, surely, sublimated into walks and poems, like those vague, erotic dreams that tortured me at night, that always ended in a gang rape, followed by the battle of a lion and a horse on a rooftop, after which they would fall clenched together onto the ground and turn into a princely pair of embracing lovers.

Yes. Yes, I had to say again, overwhelmed by another wave of images. I remembered Dimitra, a real Greek woman with her round, full figure, who in college showered me with an odd devotion, more than maternal, almost jealous of my other friends. Her—who in the end fell for my old boyfriend, a violinist, and took my place in his arms, and recounted to me, with a kind of nostalgic sadness, their passionate trysts in sordid elevators and on the flat roofs of apartment blocks, wanting, it seemed, to get a reaction from me, a sign, then departing with her eyes veiled by an odd dissatisfaction.

The sea broke its liquid fruits against the shore, and

a humid, salty breeze reached us. What was that sharp, irritating smell? Another warm wave of images rose from the depth, behind my wide-open eyes. I remembered Doina, my blonde friend from work, suave and starry-eyed. Her—I took pictures of her from every possible angle, trying to capture the mysterious, pure attraction her solar beauty had over me. Her—one night she was suffering so much, after her husband of ten years had left her, that I could have taken the place of a man, just to relieve her unbearable, physical pain. But I could do nothing more than caress her tear-covered cheeks, to hold her with tenderness and pity, with the bizarre feeling that we were onstage, that we were acting out a play, a drama we did not understand and in which we were supposed to do something special, something odd and dangerous, but what? When I came home from Doina's that evening, I dreamed that I was forced to make love to my mother, a kind of giant monster, filled with overwhelming tenderness.

I heard the sea thundering rhythmically at the foot of the beach. *And after all, why not?*, a kind of parallel voice echoed through me, a grave and musical gong that wanted to yank me out of my phantasmic torpor. I remembered, with a start, the pure, exhilarated pleasure I felt from tall and beautiful women I saw on the street. The bizarre impression that some of them stirred

in me, around whom I had the ineffable, odd sensation
that I was remembering the fact that they and I belonged
to a people chosen by goddesses. Vestals of the cult of
beauty, of a vast, unearthly beauty. A strange joy of recognition came over me, as though I saw in them manifestations of my own essences, successful embodiments of
unique goddesses who had once flourished over the earth
and protected it with a green and purple cloak of love and
fertility. I once partook in that host of goddesses, I felt, at
some point, on another level, in another life.

What is this silly, malicious fear, I said to myself, of
a flow that in any case you can't prevent, can't stop, that
penetrates every thing and every being, and exists in any
case without you, everywhere and in between all things,
on the earth, in the air, and in the stars, between objects
and trees and animals and people and planets and solar
systems? What is any dirtier, what is any more abnormal
in this exhilaration than in other forms of attraction? I
remembered next that in college I had a kind of passion
for another student's black leather jacket, it seemed full
of hidden meaning, in the way it hung from a hook, a
precious object, worthy of adoration, because to me it
emanated an intense emotional aura. Or my affection for
my puppy, Sessy, who stared at me with the most devoted
eyes in the world whenever she could tell I was troubled,
suffering; in her no longer animal gaze, I thought I could

see a limitless, protective force, coming through her from somewhere else, to comfort me. Or the moment when, dumped for the first time at age seventeen by a boy I was crazy about, feeling like I could jump off a bridge, I suddenly felt all of nature console me, I felt it wrap around me in a protective tenderness, even the bridge I wanted to jump from, the rushing waters underneath, the far-off trees, the sky overhead, the railway line. It all silently sent me its care, its affectionate attention. And I returned an identical affection. That is, one as vast as the world. You can love anything, in fact, you can love all of it, all of it.

On the top step of the concrete stairs, I looked at you again, darling, more closely. You were there, beside me, absent. You gazed, silent and frowning, at the enormous sound of crashing water in front of you. You seemed to expect something to appear. I also looked at the sea. The sea was there, rushing and yet calm in its predictable rhythm, and far away a whiteish shining point was visible, a ship maybe, or a larger boat, or a dolphin, it seemed to approach the shore with some speed. Then it seemed to me that the sea was rising, along with the shining dot, it seemed to be coming toward me, to be rising, rushing over the shore and trying to climb my legs, toward my chest, to cover me with a dark wave. For a moment, I felt intensely afraid, for a moment my mind dissolved. Then I felt the top of my head flooded with a certain warm light and gentle immensity. I felt full of your love and the love of all my old and hidden images, come suddenly to the surface, like a froth of waves, purified and fecund.

I felt that I could encompass everything within me. The salty seawater and the translucid, gray clouds above. And the enormous noise of the waves and the strident cries of the gulls darting over the sea. And the noisy kids playing at the end of the concrete stairs, and the old people wandering down the boardwalk, breathing in the salty afternoon air. Even the empty plastic cups, even the paper thrown away in the dry grass. I felt I could encompass even the women at the other end of the concrete steps.

Alongside you, looking silently at the sea, there was room for the two women, and all people, we were all the same living material in various shapes, energized differently by the same vast, erotic electricity, an aerial sea of dancing, invisible electrons, lovingly penetrating all living creatures: a free and encompassing embrace, an intoxicating breath, a wave that rises anywhere and serves anyone and surmounts any barrier, any prohibition or limitation, because it does not belong to the person but to the world, to the cosmos, to the total intelligence. And embracing everything, it embraces itself, and it loves itself forever.

I looked at the sea. I felt that, in the end, something like a stiff cord had broken inside my chest. The stream of interior images had stopped. I felt purified. I breathed the cool and salty air in deeply. I was at last free. Free. Liberated. Now we could leave. When we got up, I looked down again at the other end of the steps, but the two young women had left. I saw them farther away, on the levy, holding hands, their dresses blown by the strong breeze. There was still a naturalness in their motions, a kind of childishness, a naïvety. Maybe they actually were sisters, classmates, students, friends. Around them, the waves continued to land with their massive, enormous sound, the pure, fecund saliva of a gigantic liquid mammal.

What smelled so strange, so sharp and aggravating, so wet and encompassing? What was that smell? A woman. A vast, all-encompassing woman.

THE CHURCH OF AIR

That is how it was, darling, at the time. Maybe you won't believe it, but I am only describing what I actually saw—what I saw—and what you think I only dreamed. If you make me explain or analyze this story, it will roll up, will darken and die, in comparison with your lucidity it means hardly anything, it's absurd. But if you are silent and listen and you begin to vibrate, if you let yourself be caught up in the net and something inside you melts, then your recalcitrant mind will quiet and silence and you will begin to see.

That day, the two of us decided, my friend Anca, whom you know, and I, to do what we had wanted to do when we were in college. We set out one morning in our provincial town of rotting, medieval ivy. We walked together down the asphalt; the dew-wet street was like an opaque, ashen mirror that the silent sun was just beginning to make shine.

The road wound between white shacks, between lots planted with corn and vineyards the color of warmed bronze; it was autumn already, as we could see in the burned faces of the leaves and in the orange light, strangely pure, that slanted over our surroundings.

We came quickly to the bottom of the hill. The pine trees that covered it were sparse, light green stripes that crossed the almost black stripes of shadow in the blue air. The road rose sharply through the pines, circling the hill in a sand-colored spiral . We encouraged each other with a few words and began to climb.

The morning was still cool. We talked about the city and the world below. You told me that you had dreamed again about the white lake, full of the round heads of unborn infants, like the fleshy buds of yet-unopened lilies, floating silently over waves of water, a horrifying dream. I helped you calm down, like the last time; I changed the topic. Slowly, the air around us became warmer, gentler. The sun looked like a hazy egg, like a concentration of gold, seen through a wide, glass sphere, wrapped in clouds.

The path was unexpectedly steep, it took us almost an hour to reach the top, where we found the old walls of the German cathedral. We caught our breath, I sat on a large, round stone, you leaned over to pick a yellow strawflower, a modest but strong-smelling blossom.

Then we walked around the cathedral, looking for the entrance. We found that there were actually two. One, tall and imposing, with thick doors of carved oak, held by large iron straps, painted black, bordered on the sides by thin columns of gray stone, and above by a semicircular archway packed with sculptures. But this door was barred with a long piece of metal and a heavy padlock. At the end of the lefthand wall we found the other entrance, a narrow, low door of rough-hewn wood, almost rotted away, under the dark shadow of a massive buttress. This door was half open; we pushed and entered.

The vast space of the cathedral was full of columns and cool air, a dry cool, and overwhelmed by light from above. Through the high, narrow windows, shafts of sunlight fell, full of dust, colored by the simple stained glass, with almost naïve patterns. An unexpected throng of long, multicolored flags hung without moving, showing medieval family crests. Then we both looked up; the stone ogives intersected harmoniously at a great height, in a dome that looked like the hull of a giant ship, turned upside down over our small world. You began to tell me about the cathedral. I listened to your whispering lips.

Then from nowhere, a tall man appeared, dressed entirely in black. He stepped quickly toward us, greeted us with a proper politeness, and suddenly also began to explain about the planes and domes, the pillars, buttresses, capitals. Yes, yes, a Romanesque basilica with three naves, finished much later, in the Gothic period. Yes, and the square choir area, domed in a cross and finished with a semicircular apse covered by a quarter-sphere conch, a rarity. Yes, yes, thirteenth-century, here in the wasteland, at the edge of the world, yes, a German colony. Ah, and the entryway, a wonder, such a rich detail, what imposing stone décor, almost delicate as lace, Weinland influences, of course.

You were caught in a scholarly discussion with the cathedral custodian. I moved off, staring at the narrow, tall windows in the apse. Yes, the floral elements in the sculpted interior decorations, the rose, the rosette, the mystical rose with a hundred petals, symbol of Mary, the pure, the immaculate, repeated throughout the vast cathedral. You were beginning to outpace the custodian's knowledge, you remembered our college courses well, details about the cult of the most-pure Virgin, queen of heaven, flower of flowers, mother of the true man and bride of her own son born of eternity, oh, the gentleness and goodness of the world, earthly love and universal compassion, oh, the rose born in her sinless breast, the apocalyptic rose, the salvation of this vulgar world . . .

I lost myself in the sacristy, I had been pulled in by the purple color of a rotting flag I had seen through the doorway. And in the east wall, in the time-yellowed plaster, I spotted a bizarre crack, one that unraveled in narrow volutes that, it seemed to me, described a trembling, unsteady rose. Below the rose on the wall, in haste, I scribbled a name.

Ah, but you know everything about this place, I heard the man in black exclaim, perhaps with a bit of irritation. Why was it you said you hiked up here?

You called me over at that point, and pulling me aside, you asked in a low voice: why did we come here? Ah, yes, we came here to become nuns.

Wasn't there a convent here? Yes, yes, the custodian responded, a bit surprised. There was, but a long time ago, hundreds of years ago, and then, you with all your knowledge about Gothic and Romanesque art, you have such an education, such scientific knowledge, and you are young and beautiful, what else do you need?

Yes, what else do we need, that was the question. In fact, we only came to see the building, you said, looking at me crossly, the idea of becoming nuns came to us along the way, out of the blue, as we were struggling to get up the hill. The man in black left us alone, he went into the sacristy. We were quiet, amazed at ourselves, what had come over us?

Then you went to look at the decoration on one of the medieval flags, and I went to the apse, I wanted to see the window at the most eastward end of the cathedral. I looked, then I called to you, loudly, loudly. You came quickly, wondering what it was, and, as you were coming closer, I saw, amazed, how a kind of floral fire danced across your face, lights and shadows in concentric circles, like translucid, rustling petals, almost erupting from the features of your face, so harmonious and impenetrable, as you approached. It was only the dance of the lights that passed between the rotted flags, which a sudden current of air had moved. You asked again, amazed and a little frightened: did we actually come here to become nuns?

I didn't answer, I nodded my head toward the window. The overwhelming light came through the narrow gaps in the stone, because the window faced east. You looked. At first you did not see anything, only the long rays of light, rainbows and pointed shafts tossing refractions in every direction, crystals with brilliant facets, dust and blinding motes. I put an arm around your shoulder and pointed at something in the window. Then you saw. In the distance, there were white clouds shaped like rosebuds and lilies, opening in gentle explosions of cotton with round outlines, approaching us slowly. Below, far away, where the city was, almost nothing was visible, only a faraway whiteness, punctuated by small, variously colored right angles, triangles and squares, like a dispersed kaleidoscope sliding swiftly backward.

The sun came toward us with dizzying speed, unfolding its millions of petals tumultuously, spouting in jets of frothy light, rivers and waterfalls of flames exploding in concentric waves, approaching our tall window with its blinding rose.

And under the Romanesque-Gothic basilica, white as a bride's veil or a nun's betrothed to heaven alone, unfurling its wings in the golden, cool air, under our basilica, instead of the city there was—intensely blue, luminously azure, like a great depth, transparent and quiet—nothing but sky.

IMAGES

Darling, only when these images live vividly inside of you will anything happen. It's like a grain of wheat, long hidden in the warm alluvium of your deep and forgotten interior, that sprouts and grows and crosses the carcass of your being with its thin, green thread and rises and pierces the limit of your body and rises from the dark toward the light, however deep it was buried and however far you may be from the sun. The green thread rises and rises and lengthens and flowers and goes to seed; and the stem is odd, it is green-gold and glows with a kind of aura. From the seeds of grain, neatly arranged one beside the other and sprouting like minuscule, pointed breasts, come vertical threads of light. If you eat the grains of wheat, you will be filled with wondrous images, themselves full of ever more vivid images, like stems full of seeds, which will also be full of other images of a little-known nature.

•

Darling, I must continue to tell you these stories. I have to discharge these odd, haunting visions, as they condense memories and perceptions from times and planes I do not know and cannot master. I need to see the line of intense, special moments again, and I need to have the courage to live them over again, not just in my common, banal memory, but in a deeper memory, vaster, open to dizzying perceptions. In a parallel and yet true reality, just as true as the world outside. An intense and full reality, I ought to call it vital. A kind of depth that belongs to me but on a higher level. A kind of stellar underground. In that point inside me, hidden behind my sternum, that awakens at times and begins to gently pulse, to glow. That point, like a minuscule sun in my chest, which I can sometimes access by emptying myself of worries and thoughts, when I am able to concentrate on it in an indirect, gentle, and all-encompassing way. That glowing point that fills me with a softened magic, a spell that dissolves my awareness of my surroundings and subjects me to an intense and loving vibration, which unites me with heaven, with the galaxies.

To describe in order to understand these intense moments. Why they happened to me. And what they want to say. And why they must happen to us. And what that point is, in my chest, behind my sternum. Because something in those moments surpasses my current state of readiness and my current powers of understanding. Something like a nuclear energy of emotion,

I feel I can say, wants to erupt in them. It wants to express itself, to spray forth outside and to ignite vivid, powerful images on a plane of being that we must discover, we must access.

FOUR MOMENTS IN SPRING

1. Me

"Should I take off my clothes?" the woman asks through her teeth, watching the other man walk away leisurely, his hands in the pockets of his very white shorts.

"Of course. Why? Are you embarrassed by the him?" he answers over his shoulder, opening the zipper of his faded jeans, ripped in the knees, and removing his legs one by one. Naked, he throws his watch onto the sheet and runs toward the sea.

Clearly, she says to herself, this is why I came. With soft and unsure motions, her eyes on the two men, she takes off her long, white skirt, pulls her red T-shirt over her head, then, still staring at them, she takes off her black swimsuit.

There she is: pinkish skin, sensitive, dilated pores. The sand is already hot, almost burning. The towel is warm and velvety. There is almost no one around. The beach is almost barren. A few people in the distance. A piece of paper in the wind tumbles among the yellow-gray dunes nearby. A few dusty thistles. And the foam, yellow-white, fairly dirty, at the edge of the sea. Hot, quite hot, hot like gold that's melted and evaporated. Pretty. Nice. Peaceful. She looks at sky. A quiet, azure ocean. An aerial sea over the sea of water. To be suspended between sea and sky, without the landmark of the earth. Like in another world. Eyes tightly shut. To think of nothing.

She turns to hear the crash of the water and the guttural shouts of the two men. Dark rose color beneath the eyelids, velvet obscurity, full of gold arabesques. A kind of undulating nothing. A gentle, restful nothing. But what if there were no more nothing? But what if they weren't any more, the two men in the sea? But what if, suddenly, in this giant world there were only me, me, me, me alone, on a barren beach, in a barren world, in the universe emptied of beings, things, and events, purified, liberated of all shapes, of all these tiresome sounds, ah, of all this extenuated insanity? Yes, only this gentle, rose-colored darkness under the eyelids, this good, restful nothing, where there is only me. Me. Me. Me.

And suddenly everything was me.

The towel was me.

The sand was me.

The warm and trembling air was me, Me.

The far-off foam of the sea was me, me Me, Me.

The very blue sky, very high, ah, the sky, was me, me Me, Me, Me.

The entire world was Me, Me, Me, Me, Me, Me, M e. M e. M E. M. E. M . E. M. E. M. E . M .E . M . E . M. E. M. E. M. E.

But who is the world? The world is Me. Myself expanded, poured out, spread from my mind outward, my thought as big as the world, pure consciousness, vast, flowing in all directions, filling everything up, without limits, without borders. But who is Me? Me is the world, I am the world, the world is suddenly equal to my mind, a fistful of lucid and vivid consciousness, which coincides within my cranium, stupefying, exhilarating, with the sky and sea, with the universe, with the infinite. I am the extremely blue sky, I extend my dome over the world. I am the salty and noisy water of the sea, I crash over this and that. I am the breeze that moves the paper I am the yellow-white foam that shatters on the shore I am the warm airI am the burning sandI am the paper blowing in the windI am the swimsuits and softtowelsI am IamI IamYou IamAllofyouIamAllI am AllAll AllA L L A L L A L L A L L AL L   L

L   L   L   L   L   L   L   L

0 0 0 0 0 0 0 0 0 0 0 0 0 0 0 0 0 0 0 0 0 0 0 0 0 0 0 0 0 0 0 0 0 0 0 0 0 0 0 0 0 0 0 0

Hot. Very hot. The towel soft, velvety. The sand fine

and burning. The noise of the waves, powerful, faraway, faraway. The sea flows within and flows without. All is a sea. A sea of me. An endless field of water, of pure, blinding blue. An ocean without beginning or end.

The two men come running back, shaking off the salt water noisily. "We saw a dead baby dolphin," says one.

And? the woman says to herself.

I am the dead baby dolphin.   And the sea-foam.

I am the sand.   I am the water of the sea.   I am the sky and sun. I am the cosmos and stars. *I am. I AM.   I A M .*

2. The Third Presence

Like a lazy mollusk, the young woman awoke slowly, feeling pampered and finally fulfilled. She stretched her bare legs over the duvet, then she rolled from one side to the other, her whole body enjoying the fresh coolness of the sheets. Slowly, gingerly, she stood and moved toward the bathroom. Without a thought in her mind, like a jellyfish pulled from the water. She touched her arms, her stomach, she touched the elastic softness of her breasts, and, satisfied with what she felt, she turned the shower on.

Drenched in love, she whispered to herself and rubbed her skin with a wet sponge. Her flesh felt like a lump of dough, thoroughly kneaded by skilled hands, then left to rise. She nibbled on her arm, she slapped her thighs, and a gently painful shiver of pleasure brought everything back to her mind. She saw the previous night of love again, as though under an intensely colorful shower of images.

She relived the strange losses of self, trembling gently from the dizzying fall both of them had taken into a muscular and dark-red chaos, shaken by small waves and earthquakes—short, spasmodic. That gentle heat, from an unknown source, had stretched from a point low in her body and risen like the tide in fine, warm waves, ever more intense, through her thighs, her abdomen, her diaphragm, up to her chest, inflaming her senses, even her mind, in a kind of darkness, a gently frightening loss of self. Then a lost floating, suspended somehow, had dissolved into a void that tasted sweet and bloody, where there was nothing aside from a rhythmic pulsation: a voluptuousness turned in on itself, like a caress that caresses itself and caresses another caress, where no one knows who gives and who receives, or who is who.

And suddenly, she remembered more unclearly, more diffusely, as though projected onto a screen behind her thought, how something that had surprised them both emerged at a certain moment, they had felt *a third pres-ence* appear somehow between them, from them, or with and beside them. Something, someone had floated and wrapped itself around them. A kind of warm and attentive breath had caressed itself through them and loved itself in their interwoven arms. A faceless someone seemed to look at them in joy, invisibly insinuated along their embrac-ing bodies, without embarrassment, just the opposite, exalting their ardor. As though their motions had no lon-ger been chaotic, purely instinctive and passionate, but the start of an old, bizarre ritual, discovered by accident or a stroke of great luck. It had danced with attentive and slow movements, which they themselves had watched, some-what amazed and somewhat detached, since they had the strange impression that together they described something particular in space, almost writing something, a hieroglyph in the air—and this, this had conjured that invisible, ten-der presence alongside them. It had wrapped itself around them, dictating their motions and cadence, uniting them more tightly with its aerial embrace—and through it, their embrace had become harmonious and meaningful, a joy-ful and complete act: a partial liberation from the body, a rhythmic purification of the heart, a flashing sublimation of the mind, a heightening, a leap.

Through *that presence*, odd but gentle, the woman now understood, all that writhing of skins and muscles, those sensations and appetites and emotional short-circuits—that had taken her to pointed peaks as well as thrown her into damp, jagged gorges, shattering the colorful darkness inside her into a matter made of flame—all that writhing of skin and flesh, of tactilities and smells, of moans and short cries, all the animalistic struggle, full of claws and bird wings, took on, in her memory, an unexpectedly pure taste, clean, yet full of ardor.

Incredible, ineffable, she murmured, as she emerged from the bathroom, finally fulfilled, throwing a white, plush robe over her shoulders. Then she opened the glass doors of the balcony. And the cool of the morning struck her directly on her bare abdomen. Her abdomen vibrated like a round gong of heavy bronze, and she shivered. And the gong in her abdomen awoke a smaller silver gong in her solar plexus, which vibrated with a slightly higher and sweeter tone. And its odd warmth flowered like a delicate, white lily, behind her sternum.

And as the lily opened slowly inside her, it seemed to the woman that she was finally *feeling* her life. That she understood it. Her entire life. She felt it and encompassed it, as it connected her to all of it. Life, in all of its finally fulfilled femininity, feeling it palpitate far away, over the entire planet, like a living intelligent film, like a fecund and turbulent tide, a wave filling the gulfs and lagoons, throwing pinkish waters full of jellyfish and algae onto completely barren beaches, pouring over just-sown fields, climbing the sides of snowy mountains and leaving calcified traces on the cliffs, stretching like an enormous, soft tongue toward the horizon, climbing, climbing, reaching a sunlit peak—then retreating, like a slow undertow, from the luminous sheets of the clouds, from the now green points of the mountains, from the now full fields of rich harvests, into the lagoons and gulfs loaded with ships and people, then into the warm waters of the sea, then into the depths, into fish and jellyfish, into bacteria, into loam—a gentle undertow, like a special warmth, descending slowly down the hair, the eyes, the lips, throat, breasts, then back behind the sternum, then into the abdomen, as though it were washing the body, cooling it, purifying it, leaving it behind, as though it had decided, with difficulty, with regret, to disappear. An undertow that withdrew its limitless consciousness, that retreated from the body, over the balcony railing, toward the horizon, toward the greater world, and gave the living film back to the planets and stars.

In the high air, illuminated by the aurora borealis, with rosy fingers.

3. The Divine Gaze

On the green park bench.

Peace. Say it to myself as often as possible. Peace. Peace. Breathing deeply. Deeply. Hmm, like that. To feel its coolness in the lungs' alveoli, in the cells, in the blood. Peace. Peace. This long afternoon is strangely limpid, like a transparent, white-yellow crystal, I can see through it like dew. Amazingly pure. High sky, pearly blue-violet. Orange light, warm and slanted. I should be pure for this light, perfectly pure, I should be transparent.

Peace. To not think of anything. To only look. To look for a long time. To truly *see*. The windows in the apartment block across the park glitter a metallic green, through the windblown curtains. And the peonies near my bench are so purple, almost blood-colored, living blood, coagulated, such that their image hurts my eyes. I am afraid I will fall into their soft, velvety depth. It palpitates, it calls me so intensely. But what is intensity?

Let's see. Let's feel. It is a calm, peaceful gaze. Detached, pure, precise. That falls into the middle of things. An attentive gaze. Extremely attentive. So attentive, like an emotional laser, it could turn into peonies. Into their perfumed and bloody inflorescence. Into their velvet explosion.

Peace. Peace. Say it often. As though I were casting a

spell, as though I were praying. Breathing deeply. Deeply. Deeply. To feel its coolness in my cells. In that place in the box of my chest, where something once moved, vibrated, like a little rosette of rapidly spinning air, like butterfly wings beating. The place behind my sternum.

But what if I repeated the peony petal experiment with everything I see around me? To stare at them, to think of nothing but what I see. To let my gaze dissolve into everything that is visible and to pull myself into dissolution. In fact, to let *another gaze*, something vaster, pass through me, through my eyes, and see. To be the glittering windows behind the curtains. Metallic green. Liquefied crystal. And this calm, odd clarity. And the ashen walls, so expressive now, of the buildings. And this slightly darkened foliage, alive, of the trees. Breathing deeply. Peace. Peace.

Yes, it is possible, POSSIBLE. To gaze intensely. As though I were casting, as though I were praying. To shake myself slowly from the leaves and to fall in fine particles of dust and smoke from the brow of the tall and haughty woman passing now down the path. I tremble indecisively in the gentle breeze that has begun to move the newspapers on the corner stand. To fall onto the pink and white ice cream of the boy whose hand that older man holds, as they stand in line for the cotton candy machine. To flow with the water along the gutter at the edge of the street, taking up the torn bits of paper and soggy cigarette butts. To stretch calmly along the lascivious, expansive asphalt path that stretches throughout the park. To move quickly, agilely, with the sparrow pecking nervously beside my white shoe. Yes. Yes. Peace.

Peace. Say it often, intensely. Breathing deeply. I look around myself with my attention focused like a laser. Things, objects become strangely vivid, vibrating, ready to explode in my eyes. Clear, extremely clear, with almost knifelike edges, like broken glass, like crystal shining in the colors of the rainbow. Intense and deep, abyssal. As though within them were unspoken, amazing mysteries. They enter my eyes, their vision almost hurts. They look alive, they are present, attentive. As though they were not objects. As though they were much more, something almost alive, beings in their own way. Silent, but sending something immense, dizzying, important to my mind, which is beginning to expand, to rise, to grow.

If I look at them now in a certain way, at a slant, unfocused, with a slightly wider gaze, the things become something else, *something else*, just the coagulated colors, the free colors in space, the dancing hues, floating like masterful brush marks left throughout space. They are luminous, living vibrations, undulating and interweaving in the air. A purer state of matter, resonance alone, pigment alone, as though the forms existed, temporarily, only to show these colors. The full, exultant red of tulips. The deep, restful blue of the sky. The vivid, nourishing green of rustling branches. The maddening, electrifying yellow of marigolds. The stunning, deep violet of the gentians. From all the colors flows an odd type of intense trembling, a presence. Something alive, intelligent, palpitating, something that unfolds in all the shapes around it, like disturbing mouths of various kinds whispering something, attracting, calling, inviting. Everything seems alive, there are presences around, breaths of wind full of life, the red mouths of peonies gaze at me, everything gazes into my eyes, sends me something important, gives witness to magic, to mystery.

But what if the entire world is nothing but vibration, vibration in form? What if this vibration is conscious, is a pure intelligence that evolves and gazes at itself, that embraces and loves itself? What if the entire world is nothing more than this intelligent, divine Vision? What if *the entire world is actually god*? I hear myself think, with terror. What if the trees and flowers and peonies, glittering windows, afternoon light, are—and in their way they are alive, divine—are in god? What if the boy on the path licks a piece of god and swallows a sweet and cooling god, pouring it into a small god in a pair of shorts? What if the living, vibrating bench where I sit is in god? What if the newsstand, the bronze face of the grandfather, and the line where people wait and all that is around me was at some point in the divine mind, in the abyss of innumerable possibilities of the cosmic imagination, and they are intelligent and living energy, and are now in my mind, suddenly endless, full of this holiness?

And if I am looking at the world, here and now, with *the gaze of god*? And if even I, even I, even I am, I am, I am, and I am somehow, in a way, in a mysterious way, a small, a small god, who has forgotten she is god?

4. The Other World

The buzzing wasps were louder, almost metallic, over the park flowerbeds. Wasps or bees? The viscous, humid heat of the afternoon became even more oppressive. Suddenly, the woman emerged from the somnolence into which she had fallen. She opened her eyes slowly. The bright, orange-gold light fell in slanted bands over the bench. The heavy, viscous heat made her short hair stick to her sweaty neck. She felt fine alone, on the now hot bench. Such light, such heat, the smell of flowers just trampled by children playing nearby. The sweet murmur of birds and insects moving among the green-painted benches and wooden newsstands.

What splendor, what joy! The woman allowed herself to be drenched again in these sensations. Without
thoughts. Without any thought of the world outside. Just
like last year, someone inside her whispers in her ear. Just
like two years ago and ten years ago. Just like every year,
here in the park, in summer, with the trees and flowers.
The same violent sensations, sweet, melting. Of joy, of
wonder. Paradisiacal. Without time. Ah, without time,
without hours, without minutes, without a schedule,
without morning or evening. Just like always. Just like
in childhood. Just like in *the other world*. Nothing inside,
in the essence of her being, she said to herself, it's like
nothing has changed. The same hunger. Everything is the
same. Identical to itself. The same sweetness, heavy, unctuous, to the point of satiety, to the point that the too-
good is a kind of evil. As though you could suffocate, as
though you could die of splendor.

And suddenly, in the middle of this joy delectated
without haste, on the bench in the middle of the park, a
wave of disgust and nausea washed over her. As though,
without warning, a wave of milk burst through the
blouse of a woman who had not known she was pregnant, a seed that was growing inside her and consuming
her substance, in order to extend it past the cliff face of
time. Or as though a wave of dark terror took hold of

you, alongside your beloved, lying in a deep sleep after a night of love, from too much ardor.

And the woman suddenly understood, but how?, that this melted sweetness of the senses, so intense she almost didn't feel her own body any longer, this green-gold light, this smell of warmed peonies, the buzzing of wasps or bees, this pure joy with which she regarded everything around her, everything, everything, in this limpid moment outside of time—precisely all of this was the taste of death.

Her complete and weighty intuition. Supremely frightening yet deeply joyful. All this was death's sign, was its welcome gift. The gold-framed mirror where death let itself be seen. The enormous, fabulous spectacle death produced with an astounding waste of materials, colorful and alive, in front of her tear-wet eyes. It was its great dance through the air, over the earth and the waters, just for her, who sat on the bench at this moment in a lazy position, so she could see, little by little, through the waves of the spectacle, something. To understand. To accept. To be exhilarated. To let herself be taken. To outgrow this being. That is, *to be*. To be All, finally, and for once.

Just as, through its burning, the pyre transforms into luminous ash and into splendor. Just as through its inner chemistry any suffering, even physical, can become the opportunity for awakening and joy. Because this carnivorous world, this crude and loving universe extracts its ecstasies through its own fastidious destruction. And through ecstasy it recompenses its victims as it completes its disasters. And through ecstasy something comes, a unifying vibration, a mental geyser, a bridge to *the other world*.

The woman heard the wasps buzzing more intensely over her head, she felt the sweet-painful, liquefied, viscous heat. The slanted light, orange-gold, and the summer, the summer like an exhilarated apocalypse. Like a simple and no less amazing revelation. Raising her gaze toward the tall trees around her, she saw a bizarrely shaped leaf, like a streaked fan, milky green, falling slowly, like paper, from a gingko tree. A leaf gently yellowed by the sun. And seeing it, her mind opened and she understood in a flash, as though within a new limitlessness, that that leaf had been falling, slowly, rocking, since the beginning of the world. It was falling, it fell, it still fell and still fell from eternity.

WHORE

Darling, you have provided me more than enough time to think of my next story. You left me here and went to take a turn through town. Probably you're in a bar somewhere, "with the boys." You're having a beer or a vodka. Solving all the country's problems, hearing the latest, the word on the street. You're ranking writers, naming the best poet, best novelist, who earns the most with movies or plays, who is on television most often or interviewed on the radio and so on. But especially, who is sleeping with whom.

Ah, that's it, that's the hottest topic. What fresh meat has appeared on the horizon, students in literature, or foreign languages, or a few picked from the odder departments, atomic physics, art history, or electrical engineering. The hottie with the best boobs or longest legs. The babe with the curliest and shiniest hair, or the fleshiest lips. The girl with the best clothes or best makeup. With the hottest and roundest hips or the finest calves. With the best nipples pointing through her blouse. The most uninhibited girl and the most popular. The cutest girl, the most democratic. Ah, but she's a whore, she sleeps with everybody. How do you know? I saw her with this guy. That's what people say. She even slept with me. And how was it, how was it? It was how it was, but afterward she told me about her first guy, her great love, who dumped her and now she doesn't give a care. Then, can you believe it, she left the room in the hotel where we were, she threw a few clothes on and walked out, went down to the bar, bought a round for everyone and got stinking, stinking drunk! I dumped her, too. A cunt, a slut, a whore. Yes, a whore, a little whore . . .

Darling, I've been waiting for you for a while, but you and your boys are probably debating your sexual rankings over a beer, a vodka. Which male is the wildest, the most potent, the toughest, who's had the most women. Who and when. What and where. You're telling hot little stories. Ingenious positions, what you did and what you told her. You're laughing loud, rolling around, in the hormonal abyss. You could sleep with every woman, you could get stinking drunk and fall under the table, you could dirty any girl who passes, imagining how good she'd be in bed, and still, still, you would never be prostitutes, hookers, hussies, whores, sluts. That's how you think, as you order another round of beer or vodka, chuckling together, slapping each other on the shoulders. While your fiancée, your lover, your pure and well-behaved wife is waiting for you at home. That's how you think.

My darling, that cute little whore could be me. Or her, or

any other woman. Her, who will have to pass through a series
of men, through their rough, rushed, unskilled hands, through
their vain, hungry mouths, through their imaginary and
abstract cortex, through the bizarre limits they create at every
step; she will have to free herself of this enormous fear, stupid-
ity, terror, connected to the soft, pink portal under her skirt,
between her legs, what is done and what is not, what is good
and what is bad, what her mother says and what her father
thinks, with fear for how people talk and what the local author-
ities will see; she will have to fall, to fall and fall, through hotel
beds and beds in respectable families' houses, through dorm
rooms and borrowed studios, through elevators and public toi-
lets and block rooftops, to fall and fall, in her own eyes and in the
eyes of those who know, innumerable eyes, into incoherent frag-
ments of mistaken experiences, of furtive embraces and illegal
loves, impossible, aberrant; horrified by her starving body and
at the same time frightened of hell, wishing to be mary magda-
lene and the holy virgin, feeling like a whore, and goddess, and
child, and matron, and sometimes even a man; under as many
prohibitions as they could think of, those grandmothers and
teachers and neighbors, under so many temptations that she
could bleed romance novels, CDs of sentimental music, soft-core
porn DVDs, and steamy stories she heard from other people;
impossible to be a virgin in a world obsessed with sex, impreg-
nated with sex, founded on sex, since as a child and a teen-
ager her mind was bombarded with obscenities on the street and

lascivious images in Playboys glanced at in her father's desk or on porn videos lent by friends; and still, she always and always feels irreducibly and irrevocably pure, innocent, chaste, and immaculate like the Holy Virgin in her sweet-painful nucleus in the unknown abyss, closed in her feminine body.

In this female body and hidden being, ignored and scorned within, I once felt, some time ago, watching you by chance on the street as you were passionately kissing another woman, you, the exigent and the moral, full of judgments and verdicts, I felt, in front of your passionate and free embrace, after the first, fleeting impulses of jealousy and pain, I felt how something inside me activated a central, round place, how behind my sternum a small emotional sphere heated up, one about the size of a red-gold apple, and from this sphere, whirling quickly as it grew and opened rapidly in a kind of rosette, an interior flower, from its petals and its engorged pistil of future fruit, toward you two and toward the world jetted a warm, undulating wave of a more comprehensive love, vaster. And this is also a bridge toward the other world.

Darling, that pained and scorned whore, any woman, could be me.

THE ENORMOUS WOMAN

For some time, the image of an enormous woman has followed me. I see her on waking, a baggy, white blur, someone at the back of my eyes, like a vague decoration hung on other images from the crowd that continuously parades across my mind. I catch myself thinking about bold, fat women from the park or the stores or from the street. I look at them with an unhealthy insistence, too brazen. I do not know what both attracts me to them and irritates me. I once thought of a very short story, in which a woman who sells bus tickets, named Duda, starts to gain weight after her husband leaves her, more weight, and more weight, until she can't get out of her little ticket booth of green-painted metal.

In fact, I'm not doing so well with myself, that's how it is, since I'm not doing so well with you. Detested, beloved, odious, adored man. Animal in jeans and sneakers. God in a T-shirt and leather jacket, full of appetites and manias, pride and weakness. One evening as I was suffering from this continual struggle with someone who could be from a different kingdom than me, something happened to me, a terrible thing:

I was in a bus, fairly empty at that hour. Only a few men and two or three women on the brown plastic benches. I am alone in a double seat with scratched backs, one of them is cracked down the middle, exposing the metal structure underneath. I am going to visit my mother, who lives in an apartment in another neighborhood. At one stop, a corpulent, obese, woman struggles to climb up into the bus, with her load of shopping bags. She seems vaguely familiar, although her face is banal, crude, expressionless. Still, I think I have seen her somewhere. The woman sits right next to me. It bothers me, there are free seats nearby, she could have sat somewhere else. A wave of irritation tenses the muscles in my diaphragm.

This large and powerful woman. These enormous, overwhelming women. Not like me, skinny as I am. My mother, for example, comes to mind, a willful and rough woman, a kind of female man, an army commander, energetic, arms as strong as two men put together, who tortured me from a very young age with her inflexible will, pressed me to become what she wanted, something that she could not or did not have the courage to be. Or our nanny, Victorița, another force of nature, with her child made with who knows whom and raised in an orphanage, with her drunken, tearful hysterias, with her heavy slaps whenever I deviated in any way from the daily rituals of washing, eating, studying, sleeping, when my mother was not home and could not see her hit me.

These large women, overwhelming, terrible. Elenore, for example, my possessive spinster aunt, heavy but well-dressed and well-coiffed, with her overbleached blond hair, who insisted I learn French and that she would make me a "lady." Mara, my grandmother's sister, a Catholic nun, who came to stay with us when her convent was shut down: wide as a cabinet and always dressed in her black, smelly cassock, she forced me to sleep next to her in the mornings and she suffocated me with maternal embraces while she mechanically recited her little prayers. Or my boss at the office, an acrid mountain of flesh full of pretentiousness and anger. Finally, my thoughts returned furiously to the bus, to the woman next to me, and a wave of irritated and powerless heat overcame me and I slid to the other side.

Then I saw the terrible woman who had appeared in my dream. A giant, enormous woman. She was right in the center of the world, on a kind of old stone stool, and around her the sky rotated its glittering constellations. She was naked, she was monstrous, a heap of muscles and pleats and folds of fat and flesh, with innumerable overlapping breasts like long, thick scales, like innumerable bunches of grapes with long, violet nipples, from her wide chest down to her stomach. And under her large and wavy stomach, from her hidden, shadowy triangle, as though through a majestic temple gate of warm marble, a stream of people poured out and a stream of people entered, like dark ants, myriads and myriads of ants. The woman held the earth in her lap and fed it streams of milk cascading from her innumerable mammaries, but at the same time she almost enveloped and suffocated the world with her folds of heavy, overwhelming flesh. She was giant and dark, like the outline of a rosy mountain against a violet, far-off sky. She huffed and she gurgled from her thick layers of flesh and waves of fat and hair-covered skin wet with discolored strands and tiny brown freckles. From time to time she grabbed a handful of people and shoved them inside her wide, thick-lipped mouth, curved like a bloody, horizontal figure eight. She ate them up hungrily. But below, other people came out of her, more people, innumerable people. She was an infernal blender, a rock- and metal-melting oven inside of whom was a visible stretch of bloody flesh, red-hot and liquid.

Something frightening and unbearable in this image fascinates me. Something ineffable attracts me, I approach that body fearfully, it looks like a warm, soft mountain, that seems to hold up the sky with its head and fill the world with its sweaty flesh, dark and plentiful, set on its stone stool, with its back to the glittering constellations that draw a pale halo in the sky around her shape. I felt horribly attracted, I could have gone toward her, to press myself to her body, I could have entered her, made love with that archaic monster, died from such pleasure, like a flea crushed by an elephant, like a mouse caught in an erupting volcano. And a kind of strong wind tore me from my far-off vantage point, a kind of invincible magnetism pushed me toward her, pressed me against her plentiful, palpitating flesh, and crushed me.

I am on the bus again. Disgust and fear remain in my body after the vision of the immense woman. I feel sweaty, my dress sticks to my body. I look out of the corner of my eye at the woman in the seat next to me. A monster, I say again to myself, so obese, her overflowing hams, her wide face, her figure drowning in fat—they all remind me of someone. But who? And then the woman begins to crowd into me. As though she wants to come closer, so she won't fall off the chair, or perhaps she feels protected by me. Or she wants comfort, or to come on to me, like a man, with vulgar, precise advances. She crowds me, she winks, and her hideous face smiles gallantly, she laughs toward me slowly. I squeeze against the side of the bus until I run out of space. I feel crushed. I feel disgusted and scared. An awful fear manipulates the walls of my stomach. I want to say something, to scream, to revolt. I want to motion to the others in the bus, but the fear is too sudden and the fear of ridicule stops me, mutes me. I want to get up, to change my place, to flee. Or to jump off the bus that seems to be moving more and more quickly without stopping at its stations. But the fat woman holds me prisoner with her ample body, pressed firmly against me. Then, as she bounces with the bus, I am terrified that she is moving on top of me. Like a puffy duvet, wide and heavy. Like an avalanche of heavy and strangely warm snow. A black wave covers me and an overwhelming warmth falls from above. I feel I am going to die and a deep terror takes me over, mixed strangely with an intense pleasure. Dissolving, enormous.

But, in the moment I thought I would die, I realize that the giant woman resembles an enormous Buddha, sitting in meditation. She is a feminine Buddha, a giant gold statue, in the shape of a pyramid. Her head has long braids, like a woman. Her body is made in fact from multiple, superimposed women, like a tower of apartments with multiple floors, and the floors, these levels, undulate each with its own head, with its own breasts, with its own stomach. And on each head is a face, the same face, repeated identically many times. And that face, that face is actually . . . my face! That idol-monster-goddess, the monster Buddha, is me!

Then I feel revulsion, I want to scream, to yell, and suddenly I come to myself. I am drenched in a strong-smelling sweat, at once salty and acrid and bitter and sweet.

This smell reminds me of my mother.

A MESSAGE

Darling, you stare at me in disbelief, peculiar things like these don't happen to you, or maybe you just won't admit it. You won't let yourself be invaded by inner images, more intense and colorful than the world outside. Your brain isn't home to celestial or monstrous visions of stories you don't understand, that irritate you, obsess you, sometimes even anger you, but that you cannot ignore. Because they emanate a force, a magnetism that the exterior world does not have, because they seem to send an essential, vital message—encoded and obscure, it's true, because it is mostly visual—that irritates, that angers. Too many images want to say something important in an unclear and vague manner, instead of making their demands clear, fast, unequivocal. Too many visions, as though they fell from the sky or climbed out of the ocean, sending you something like a vibrating affective energy, an overwhelming emotion. Images that want to pull you from yourself, to push you somewhere higher or somewhere else, to raise you to another level of your fragmented, macerated mind, pulled in every direction. Your mind like a computer full of utilitarian, peripheral programs that do not speak to each other, that have forgotten their central program and use up heaps of energy. Your shaped, trained mind, formed to face the world in front of you, but ever more forgetful of the world inside, ever more incapable of exploring it, understanding it, reconciling itself to it. And then, this interior world, like a kind of undercolonized continent full of rare, precious metals that could give access to fabulous energies, to mental bridges that now we can only dream of, this world like a kind of forgotten land, although that is where your roots come from and perhaps, in the future, your wings, this world like a kind of great nocturnal metropolis, hidden by a wall you cannot see, full of noble palaces and residential neighborhoods but also some dangerous places of evil reputation, your interior city of parks and imposing buildings, but also empty lots and garbage pits from which phantoms, monsters, and wild beasts sometimes come, this inner world revolts, it wants to be known, recognized, accepted, transfigured, and it sends sumptuous or terrifying images, sends armies of strange, provoking images, it assaults you, it reminds you that it exists and that it has an essential message to send you . . .

But let me tell you, let me remind you, in fact, of more stories.

MORE THAN ONE
TYPE OF BODY

There are more bodies inside our body, inside our seemingly singular body, seemingly compact, sealed and finished. How can this be? Are they like the delicate, translucid layers of an onion, under its dry and red-yellow wrapper? Or like Russian dolls, one inside the other?, you ask. I do not know, darling, I cannot explain it to you logically, analytically, with cause and effect, as you might want; I collect states, visions, and experiences. That is, a kind of theory of the senses, in pain or exaltation, a kind of practical, experimental metaphysics, a more-than-physics studied and documented by means of the body—the senses, as your philosophical friends would say. But these states and experiences are something like beings, they have beginnings and ends, they appear in a flash then die, they disappear, and they move in an intermediary state, one both within and without. These experiences cannot be repeated on command, they do not come when I want them to, rather they erupt when they want, or when they can, that is, when they find a window of expression within our overly busy being. They live in a single point of time, one both intense and present. They cannot be dissected without destroying their life, their vibration; they cannot be completely analyzed without murdering the potent magic that puts you in the *state*—they can only be relived, that is, their story told.

For example, the sweet-smelling body of my mother. *Her aromal body.* As a child, I would put on my mother's nightshirt when she was away, and, breathing it in, I immediately had her entire body beside me. That certain scent, slightly thick and sweet, a mixture of folliculin and sweat and a bit of cologne, would fill me with such happiness I could faint; I didn't feel the loneliness, separation, rupture, because I had her entire body in my nostrils, and from there I had her in my senses, and from there in my heart and my little mind. To the extent that the body of scents fed me, it was a kind of milk that entered my pores through the air, it settled my hunger and thirst for my mother so I could fall asleep. I had her beside me, with me, in me. But when my father, one day, said I wasn't allowed to take my mother's shirt to bed, and he told me to be a big girl, "to grow up," it was a moment of such intense pain that I became instantly *conscious.* Something snapped within me, an invisible, perfumed umbilical cord. I never forgot this moment.

I had to give up the sweet-smelling nightshirt. I gained a moment of presence, a shard of consciousness, but I lost something vital, essential, my mother's enveloping protection was stolen from me, my mother who was the world, the entire world.

Only recently have I rediscovered that body of scent in the air around my own body. It's hard to believe, but for some time now I have been noticing my own womanly smell. A scent slightly thick and sweet, and it bothers me, its folliculin and sweat and something indecipherable, gentle, delicate, like the traces of incense. *My hormonal body.* It's like a cocoon of transparent silk around me, it meticulously connects every part of me with its thin, invisible threads, and it encloses me inexorably in my irrevocable, pupal destiny.

When I feel it about me, evident, unavoidable, I sometimes retreat into a particular mental place, I do not know how, but I always come to the same scene: I'm in a narrow green valley, at one end there is a small chalk-stone amphitheater, a beautiful light ochre color, golden. As I proceed through the valley toward the ancient amphitheater, on my left I see a naked, small girl sitting curled up on the ground, her back toward me. Her hair is short, blond, and curly. Her body is thin and fragile, I can see her delicate shoulder blades through her skin, her thin ribs, and the small nodes of her spine. I try to walk around to see her face. I do not know why, but I cannot do so.

I go farther through the valley. I come across a girl, also on my left, an adolescent, who is also curled up on the road, her back to me. She is naked, her long hair reaches her shoulders, light-satin-colored. I see her thin waist and still-thin hips, with two indentations on either side of her small sacral bone. A golden, light fur stretches along her boldly arched spine. I try to walk around to see her face, too. I do not know why, but I cannot do so.

Then, farther along the valley, I come to a young, naked woman, also sitting on the ground, her knees to her mouth and her back facing me. Her back is beautiful and muscular, yet supple and fine, and her black, straight hair falls freely to her waist. Her hips are well rounded and powerful. The shape of her body seems familiar to me. I try to walk around to see her face, but this time, too, I cannot do so.

I go farther, I walk briskly through the narrow and green valley toward the ancient amphitheater, and I am suddenly taken with a terrible nostalgia: I realize that the little girl and the adolescent and the young woman are all me. They are my past bodies, surpassed, left somewhere behind like dry, abandoned shells, like a larva's or a pupa's exuviae, preserved eternally at the bottom of a green, sad valley. Ahead I see some statues on the right with their backs to me, waiting. But where is this valley? Is it inside my brain or somehow outside, within a vaster intelligence?

There is a *body of presence*, secreted by essential, clamorous memories. Sometimes I get up in the morning thinking constantly of something very dear, and this produces a warm feeling in my chest, behind my sternum, for example I think of the yard of my grandparents' country house, the yard where I spent my summer vacations. I want to be there again, and I reimagine the place in all its details, with all its elements, but without my grandparents, since they have died. And suddenly, I do not know how, I am actually there. I'm actually there, at my grandparents' home, I have an extremely clear, hallucinatory vision of the place. In fact, I have the joyful and frightening certainty that in an ineffable way I actually am there again, in the country, because my perceptions and consciousness are so intense, but which ones?

I am in the yard behind my grandparents' house, the one covered in short, fresh green grass, like at the start of spring. It is empty, no one seems to be there, but I see the raw light of morning, I feel the fertile, wet coolness of the air, I feel the dank scent of buds on the tree branches, I see their blue shadows below, and I know for sure, for sure, that I have transported myself somehow to the place where I wanted to return. It is true, the yard seems uninhabited, as though I imagined it half-asleep, still in bed, because my ordinary and common rationality knows perfectly well that the house was sold many years ago to strangers. So I have somehow teleported, I do not know how, in my mental imagination, to my grandparents' place, which I have reconstructed as it was long ago.

Everything lasts a few long, slow seconds. Or minutes, perhaps. The strong light of spring makes me joyful and blinds me. Suddenly I am frightened by the strange intensity, much too vivid, of my presence there, within a mental projection that is clearer, truer than the reality I left behind. Next a kind of vibration travels over my body in waves and frightens me more than the fact that I was conscious of my presence there, in the virtual backyard of my grandparents. It is a vibration that I have experienced in certain dreams, or in diurnal visions and special states, it is like a bizarre electrical current, coming from accidental contact with a superior, unknown energy outlet. A vibration that frightens me every time it appears, as though my body were not prepared for this new, unknown energy. An energy, hidden perhaps in the depths of my cells, emanated from an unknown part of them, I say to myself, one which may intersect a similar but vaster energy that comes from the stars, an energy of a nature foreign to the physical forces we know.

As the vibration reaches a dizzying intensity, shaking my feverous body, I think to myself quickly, "I want to go back, I want to go back!" I find myself again in my bed, with my eyes open, without having slept at all, as though I had been in a seldom visited space in my brain, or outside of it, and then traveled back to my ordinary brain, as though I recovered (with a certain regret) from my powerful interior imagination, where all my conscious power had taken me. But what kind of consciousness?

Then there is a *body of love*. We are together in bed, we love each other, we make love. It is a kind of horizontal ballet, an unfettered dance, with set figures and free figures, I almost feel I could sing. You rub me with your hands, you shape me like a vase of wet, soft clay, I let myself be shaped, together we create the perfect work of art, an expressive and harmonious work, a work of art both whole and fleeting. I pay attention to you, all my pores receive your skilled and ardent kisses and caresses. I am here, I am with you, in you, in me, we are together, we are in the present. *We are, we actually are*. At the same time, behind my closed eyes, a film whirs, full of exhilarating, strangely clear images. I see an ancient forest of

copper-gold oak trees, rustling, undulating. In their center, I see a luminous, wide clearing, square-shaped, full
of blue-purple flowers, each as tall as a person. The flowers are very thick, their blooms are odd, complicated and
geometrical, amazingly beautiful. Within them, I see
the entrance to a conical palace, white, not very tall, and
within it I see a hall full of the most fabulous treasures,
silver and copper vases and steel weapons decorated with
silver; old, heavy jewelry; and silver and gold coins and
precious stones of every color, shining softly in the low
light. And then *I see, I see* that I have become, pure and
simple, an Egyptian sarcophagus. My shape, a vaguely
human outline, is cut into the granite. I am painted on
the outside with small men and women in poses of adoration, their arms raised, shaking palm branches toward
an unknown god. I am an open sarcophagus, but inside I
am barren, empty. There is no body, no mummy inside
me. My interior is dark and dry, open toward the abyss
above, on high. Its emptiness awaits a presence, a seed, a
being. And suddenly you fall over me, in fact you are lying
gently and surely over the sarcophagus like a rock over
the mouth of a tomb. Your shape is odd, a mixture of various animal forms. Inside are a lion and a bull and a lamb
and an angel chick. Your shape, for me, is the Sphinx. And
I understand, finally, irrevocably, that you are, for me, the
closure, your massive setting over the barren sarcophagus,

you close over, you seal a great mystery there, below, inside. A deep mystery, fecund and indescribable.

There is also a *body of lucidity*. Reclining on a chaise lounge, I close my eyes, I observe myself within my body. Better said, from the interior of my head, from the round basket of my cranium, where I try to visualize my various parts and members. My thought observes my exterior form, from the tips of my toes up, over my calves, over my knees, hips, and pubis, toward my abdomen, diaphragm, sternum, breasts, and throat, and back to my head again. When I come to the face, my thoughts caress my forehead, the shape of my cheeks, nose, mouth. I do so slowly, concentrating. I repeat the operation multiple times. After a while, a thought comes to me, I realize that *I am not this*. I am something other than this mass of flesh covered by a moist epidermis. I, *I* am somehow a little to one side and above, I am somehow detached. *I*, I am in fact trapped in a carcass of bones, skin, and muscle. I animate a large doll of living, organic material. I am held captive inside a marionette made of an odd material, a warm material that feels pain and regenerates itself. What am I doing in this mechanical doll, in this complicated machinery? Who trapped me inside?

Simply put, I am a prisoner inside a sophisticated

deep-sea diving costume. The skin is the sensitive, temperature-regulated protective layer. The senses are complicated data-collection instruments for the environment nearby, unknown and possibly hostile. The eyes are two small video cameras of unreliable quality, the images they deliver must always be corrected. Nor do smell, or hearing, or taste perform very well, they collapse, go offline. The mouth takes samples of flora and fauna and sends them to the internal processing plant. The lungs are the carburetor, there the gases are mixed for combustion. The heart is the diving costume's heat source. From there, the red liquid for feeding, repairing, cleaning, heating, and cooling lubricates the entire assemblage. The brain is the bridge control panel, its principal computer is programmed to process the technical data of innumerable sensing instruments directed toward the explorable world. There are even more sophisticated computers there, but they seem to not work, no one knows how to run them, they're forgotten in the corners. In fact, as I understand one afternoon, I have been sent to explore a strange and far-off planet. My spaceship dropped me off on this hostile planet, in a vast and unknown forest, full of ancient trees, wild animals, dark swamps, and other dangers. Okay, but how did I begin to identify with my tools, with my oh-so-sophisticated cosmic diving costume? How did I come to believe that I am only the control panel, full of screens and electric signals, that I am the instruments of perception, that I am the carburetor and the heating plant and the feeding-cooling liquid? What happened on landing? What terrible shock disrupted my connection with the main computer, left it on autopilot? How could it take my place in the cockpit in my own head? And how did I forget about the more sophisticated computers that wait, unused, in the corners? Was this somehow necessary or was it a malfunction, a "revolt of the machines," a forced disconnect order sent from the source? And how can I operate all the controls without an *I*, without an *I am*, without myself?

I hold a small dried fruit. It's the size of a large acorn, or a chestnut, its round-oval shape is also vaguely polyhedral, because of its small facets. It is late, very late, I hear from somewhere outside me, in an apodictic and definitive tone, this acorn, this chestnut, cannot be used anymore. It is an old fruit, dead and dry, it will never sprout. Yes, I admit within my being and show without, I see that the fruit is woody and dry. It is not that nice to look at. But at the same time I feel acutely that it is my fruit, I know that it is mine, *mine*, as dead and dry as it is. This fruit belongs to me in a profound way, it is a part of me, I believe in it, even if it is late, very late; I feel that this thing is important.

Then, surprisingly, that acorn, that chestnut, that ugly, dried-out fruit, makes a beautiful crack, it splits loudly, it breaks into four equal parts in the nest of my hands, damp with wonder. The four quarters of shell make a tiny cross, with the ends of the arms bent slightly inward. From there, within, in front of my stupefied eyes, a large, vividly colorful butterfly takes flight.

Perhaps people are rockets, with different launch levels or booster stages, and we have to ignite, to unleash them in sequence, to be able to escape the earth and return to the stars. Most people burn through the first stage too quickly and carelessly, and they cannot rise more than two or three meters over the long runway of the planetary airport. Others, fewer by far, can take flight and, at the second stage of combustion, can cruise around the planet like jetliners. Even fewer people can set off the third stage and escape the earth's gravity and reach interplanetary space. But only extremely few people, two or three in a century perhaps, can execute the fourth stage and leave our solar system.

I will unfurl my wings, blue silk shot through with fine veins of gold, decorated with black and white eyes like peacock feathers, I will shake the dust off my antennae, my feet, and my instrument panel, I will set my cocoon and pupa on fire and burn my previous bodies, levels, and stages, and I will leave all of you behind. I will fly, I will rocket toward the stars.

There is more than one kind of body. Those of the future.

OBSESSIONS

Darling, I know you know that in other traditions there are systems and theories of sophisticated, astral bodies, but I am only talking to you about my own, almost banal, experience, things you have probably experienced as well. What's important is that you accept them, that you admit to them, that you give them the right to exist in the illuminated room of your consciousness, because through them an indisputable and secret message is being sent to you, information with which the mortal being within you wants to make something, the life within you wants to try something, perhaps a leap, an expansion, a departure from limits, perhaps a meeting with something greater than natural intelligence or organic life. And if you do not pay enough attention to this something, if you neglect it or scoff at it or block it, if you do not admit to its existence, this something will suffer and become inflamed, or it will contract and become infected, but in the end it will not completely die and will not disappear, rather it will attempt to emerge again, in other manifestations and other images, because something necessary hides inside, your secret and indisputable necessity.

Darling, since the moment our relationship took a dangerous turn, I entered a period of inferno-paradise-purgatory, in which all kinds of dreams and visions inundate and obsess me. I have, for example, a vision of a small mental nebula. A silk cocoon, let's say, an oval shape, a diffuse, whitish fog that sits behind my eyes. It's a kind of egg or a larva, a puffy, white larva suspended somewhere in space, far away, in the cosmic depths where, through a sudden mental leap, it connects with the depths within myself. I carry it everywhere, through rooms, on the street, up stairs, in the bus station, to work, down institutional hallways. It is always in the background of my diurnal vision and somewhere in the middle of my brain, in a hidden center. It sits there, and I do not understand why this white, oval larva obsesses me so oddly. It irritates me, sometimes it angers me. It is like a minuscule nebula, like an egg whose shell hasn't completely formed. Or like a spiral around its own axis, its circular movements at the speed of light weave the cosmic cocoon glimmering faintly in the dark. Or the thought crosses my mind that it's like an unborn child floating, lonely and melancholy, in its placental sac. When I go out, these mental visions make other people seem like half-formed fetuses, they are not yet born, they have not yet reached their definitive, true form, I see them *surrounded by a kind of halo made of albumen or foam that shields them from the real world and darkens their sight. They don't even try to escape the halo, perhaps because they don't know they can, or perhaps because they have forgotten, pure and simple, how to continue being born.*

Then I have a repeating dream in which we, darling, have to move, to change homes, because our house has become too small. It's connected somehow to caring for a child, but what child can it be, since we are just two young, unmarried lovers? In the end we find an apartment that will do. It's on the top floor of a small block in a modest, unpretentious neighborhood, next-door to the building where my parents live. I am downtown, in the middle of a crowd on a street, when I suddenly remember that we have left the child in the new apartment by himself. I hurry home, very worried. I enter an ashen, sad room, and I see the child balled up on a bed, facing the wall, dressed in a T-shirt and white cotton underpants. I rush over and turn him toward me. Then I see something monstrous: he is actually a deformed, ugly dwarf, and he is both an infant and old, he has the head of a grown man, with white hair and wrinkles, on an undeveloped and spindly body, with short, twisted legs. The child is white, completely white, as though he were made of writing paper or cotton batting. The little monster cries like any child, I see the drool from his toothless mouth. In fact, he has a mental disability and holds out his arms toward me and demands my affection.

I take the child unwillingly into my arms, I pat him, then I place him back in the bed and tuck him in. With my heart heavy, pained, I talk to him and caress him. He continues to cry and complain languidly in his own unintelligible language. I feel a desperate love connects us, but I also feel a horror at this deformed creature, hidden or forgotten in the apartment, this white monster who belongs to me in a profound way. I feel I must raise him, teach him, and try to transform him into a normal being. When I go out after a dream like this one, I feel that all people are hiding a small disabled child in their depths, a forgotten child, a stunted child whining and babbling and demanding attention just when you've found a moment's peace. People seem incompletely adults, far from adults, in spite of their appearances and the competitions and death matches these appearances cause; people will need centuries, millennia, to mature and to understand that we are all the same cosmic lucidity trapped in carcasses of various colors and shapes, that we are all one.

At other times, darling, when the two of us have made up for the moment, and out of the blue I feel hope for our almost ended relationship, I see a ball floating on the waves, inside of me. The sphere is fairly large, red-gold in color, it floats on the gently undulating surface of the sea. In fact, I realize, it's a head, a human head, living and fairly handsome, a head without a body, floating, rocking, content, like a raft on the calm waters of a warm sea. There is no shore, the water seems endless in every direction. Then I find myself inside the floating head, I actually am the head. I am a happy sphere bobbing over a warm, welcoming deep, blanketed with the playful sounds of waves. I feel peace, a vast joy. All of the sea, the endless sea. And within my immense, liquid body there are many beings. I feel herds of beasts within me, running freely in every direction: nervous schools of fish, innumerable undulating jellyfish, pods of happy dolphins, coral colonies and rocking fields of algae, aggressive schools of hungry sharks, pairs of energetic whales, and many other marine creatures. Their movement within me produces physical pleasure, a tickling, an internal caress, as though I were pregnant with all the creatures of the aquatic world, as though I were a living, vast body in which everything undulates, circulates, hunts and is hunted, lives and dies. I feel enormous and reconciled, I have a body without borders, vast and deep, that contains living and dynamic multitudes within.

Then I see the floating head again, I see it from without and from farther away. It is surrounded by an orange reflection. In fact, I realize it is the moon. A large, full moon, orange-gold, bouncing gently, like a rubber ball tossed across the expanse of waters. This floating moon is in fact within my interior, inside me, I feel it there rising, climbing the sky, glowing pale, then setting. My interior is in fact a vast space that extends from the sky above, which is a calm sea of air, to the sea below, which is also a sky, a liquid, upside-down sky.

When I go out after I have this vision, I feel all people are a part of me, they are living, independent photographs of me, my fragments, my past and future moments, they are ME in all my states, ages, and powers. At some moment in the past, ineffably, I broke into pieces, I liquefied, I ran and scattered into millions and millions of shards and drops, whose living water has filled all the crevices of the earth, shaking, pairing, multiplying, eliminating themselves. Each in its own way, these living drops reflect a flash of sunlight, the same sun, the only sun, whispering each, "me," "me," "me," forgetting that they are all the cells and organs and emotions and thoughts of my body. My body is an immense universe full of minuscule people, myriads and myriads, waiting to be awakened and saved. Whom I must help to climb from the depths toward the surface, toward the head, toward consciousness, and from there, still higher, still farther, toward the sun.

How can I explain all of this to you? You'll laugh at me sardonically. I know, you want to give me another long, scientific speech, point by point, to drive these bizarre imaginations out of my head. But these images lie hidden in my depths, waiting. They jet forth onto my mental screen when certain neural connections occur, when suffering or joy or unusually intense sensations break certain internal dams, they force a psychic valve to open, they unblock certain canals between my heart and mind, and they hurl a kind of vibrating bridge over logic and rationality, over perceptions and imagination. A bridge, a trampoline, a geyser toward the kingdom of images, situated between the sky and earth, between within and without, between our material world and the subtle, cosmic world, through which perhaps the universe wants to express itself, to speak to us, and to be heard and loved.

How can I explain all of this to you? You look at me ironically, your head tilted, puffing at your cigarette with a superior air. I feel again, under your proud and closed appearance, some pain hiding beneath your toughness. I feel something like weakness and stubbornness in you, something like a fatal decision, something like a wound awakening beneath spines and scales, under your verbal snarls. You are actually more fragile than I am.

But let me keep telling you stories. In fact, as I've said, all I do is remind you, and reremind you.

A LICENTIOUS IMAGE
IN THE COSMOS

I see her through the half-open window. Across the interior
courtyard of our block, inundated with the strong summer
light. Her window has no curtains, and the glass is so clean
it glitters. The woman is making the bed. It is narrow, like
a campaign bed or a doctor's examination table. From my
angle, I can't see anything in the room but the bed. The
woman arranges the bed carefully. She puts a white duvet
across, spreads it perfectly to the edges, smooths it with
her hand. Then she disappears from the frame.

The light from outside slants over one corner of the
duvet. The woman appears again, holding a dustrag, she
cleans a few objects I cannot see beside the bed. Then she
wipes the walls, which from my distance seem white and
very clean. Almost antiseptic. She is wearing just a violet T-shirt over her thin body. A T-shirt that reaches the
middle of her skinny, weak thighs. She is brown-haired
and young, from my angle I can see only her shadow and
back. She disappears from the frame again.

The window is clean and curtainless. It glitters in the summer light. After a few minutes, the woman returns and lies down, naked and calm, on the bed. She waits politely on the white, antiseptic bed, as though she were in the hospital. I am also waiting. It is afternoon, there is a soft summer heat. Beside me, you sleep. In the room with the woman, across the courtyard, nothing happens for a while. Then a man appears. The man is blond, thin, and naked. He is young enough, I only see his muscular, well-shaped back. Quietly, he stares at the woman. Then he climbs slowly onto her, and without any preliminary motion, without a sound, he begins to make love.

No sound is heard. Nothing but the soft heat, the waves of a summer afternoon. The two people make love without caressing, without kissing hungrily. They do it precisely, without extra movements. Like a medical operation, or like an illustration in a treatise on human sexual behavior. Or like a ballet of forced and impersonal steps, a horizontal, monotone dance on a stage. Or perhaps it is more a ritual act, precise and ineffable. The two seem to know they are being watched, as though they know they are not completely alone. They perfectly complete something required, something necessary. They make love without a sound, without a lascivious gesture. Precise and clean. It is a kind of strange rehearsal of something that I think I have seen before. But what?

Beside me, you sleep. The others' window is half-open and curtainless. The window glitters in the clear summer light. The two make love and I am not embarrassed to watch them. On the contrary. I feel I must see and watch them carefully. This scene had to happen, has had to happen for a long time. I feel an odd pressure in my chest, behind my sternum.

The man makes love in silence, precisely. Neither sensual nor purely mechanical. With his eyes open, he seems absorbed in something unseen. Concentrating on a thought that takes all his attention. The woman receives the love with closed eyes, in silence, without any extra motion. Calm and detached. Her passivity is neither absent nor careless. She seems absorbed by a precise thought, one that takes all her attention. But what can they be thinking of, together?

They seem to complete something serious, important, but what? The interior courtyard is completely bare. In the other windows, not even the shadow of a person, no movement. Beside me, you roll over and breathe steadily. No one sees those two, aside from me. Their window is curtainless and glitters. And they do not hide. I feel I must look at them. I know I must. I must *see*. But what?

The external sight of carnal love. A prohibited image, censored, hard to stomach. An oddly dangerous image, charged with a heavy, venomous energy, a kind of thick sediment bubbling up from the depths to defile me, to overwhelm me. As though I saw myself from outside. As though I were being tested. As though someone wanted to study my reactions. But who? Like the time when, as an adolescent, I found myself at my friend Alina's abortion, in an isolated mountain cabin. Or when I saw, without wanting to, my father's sex, when I walked into the room where he was sleeping naked. Or at college, in the dissection theater, a class on human anatomy, when we were supposed to cut open the cadaver of a woman who still wore traces of pink lipstick and blue eyeshadow. In these moments, too, I felt I was being watched, being tested. What do I feel now, what do I feel watching the two lovers? I do not know, I do not know yet. My mind dims slightly. I am a little afraid to see, I am suddenly a little nauseous. Yet I must watch. To see what I am ready to see. To see whether *I see*.

Suddenly, in front of my disturbed and impure eyes, a shameless, rude vision appears. I see two stray dogs mating awkwardly and helplessly in the corner of a market in a small provincial town. Men come over and sit, in comfortable positions, they stare at the dogs, they laugh crudely, and in rough low voices, their words fill their mouths with spit. The women watch the scene out of the corners of their eyes, in quick glances, then walk off in a hurry, their cheeks either pale or flushed. Two stray dogs mating mechanically in silence, yet purely, like animals. In their gazes there is something humble and helpless. They complete their act following an impersonal and terrible law, under the humans' cruel gazes. And yet the two parallel worlds do not meet, however much they resemble each other, give birth to each other, soil each other. One is eternally threatened by the other. I look at the scene from up close, then from far away. I look at it calmly, I feel nothing but pity. An enormous, overwhelming pity. No, it's not that.

Then, again, suddenly, as though in a scientific documentary, playing somewhere in a dark cinema where there is no one but me, I see a flea curled around a flea, I see a butterfly desperately fluttering over a butterfly, I see a snake twisted painfully around a snake, I see a turtle moving slowly over a turtle, I see a determined crocodile perched rigidly on top of a crocodile, I see a proud, hardworking rooster leaping onto a hen, I see a frightened rabbit stuck, trembling, onto a rabbit, a donkey placed on a donkey, a stallion impetuously mounted onto a mare, a rhinoceros set ridiculously on a rhinoceros, an elephant braced heavily over an elephant. It's an uproar of cries and groans, growls and fluttering, bloody maws, claws in the air and heads driven against the ground. I see a grand, apocalyptic film, a display of universal coupling, in which all that is alive bites, stings, interpenetrates, suffers, devours, and procreates.

Then, out of all these innumerable matings flow rivers of identical offspring, endlessly, as though inside a frighteningly large, living wheel, entering into each other, exiting from each other, in an eternal, circular stream.

The women and the men appear at the end of the documentary, somewhere in a corner of the frame, like a small instinctual animal species, to whom at a certain moment something happens. Yet I cannot see what it is exactly, the scene is too fast, too short. I am alone in the dark theater. This genetic film runs ineluctably before my eyes, like a waterfall of colorful lava full of wild images. There is something tragicomic in the director's vision, or the conceiver's vision. Something has to enter into something else to produce another something else, but the respective instruments are rudimentary, and the procedure is pitiful. The reproductive organs have not been designed well—oh, far from it. They could have had more beautiful shapes, simpler shapes, nobler shapes. And people's genitals should have looked different from the animals', more elegant, if I can put it that way, they should have been designed with more equality between the sexes. Watching the film of terrestrial couplings, I feel nothing but tenderness, a feeling that softens the corners of my mouth. An immense tenderness that fills the theater and suddenly turns the image off. No, it is not that. It's not that.

Now I see a couple, a woman and a man, in a series of color photos in a pornographic magazine. The same as the one I came across in my father's desk drawer, when I had just started puberty. The couple's shiny copper flesh was probably oiled, because it glistens tantalizingly from the pages of the magazine. The muscles of the two are well sculpted. In one of the pictures, the man and woman execute a provocative erotic pose perfectly. The camera flash catches them in an exciting position, one which it seems they will repeat indifferently, endlessly. Two inflatable plastic figurines, stacked ridiculously on top of each other. Two mechanical human carcasses, covered with the best-quality skin, executing the classic crank-rod motion. Or two freshly cut hunks of meat, still warm, still streaming blood and sweat, for sale in the showcase of an upscale butcher. The image is too violent, too artificial; they are not real, they are only celluloid mannequins, there in the picture. I feel like throwing up. No. It's not that.

A husband and a wife, this time. They must conceive a child. They have wanted to for a long time, and the child has not come, in spite of their repeated, frenzied, chaotic efforts. I see them now, trapped together in a hospital room. They've run the tests. They were given a hormone treatment. Now, under the doctors' gaze, they must try to conceive a child in a scientific way, following a clear protocol. On two narrow, white, antiseptic

beds. They strive to fill their roles correctly, imperson-
ally. He deposits his sperm into a test-tube. She receives
the sperm through a long, thin, transparent tube. From
somewhere outside, electronic eyes watch them, complicated devices surround them, surgical instruments. They
are two reproductive guinea pigs, willingly subjected to
a special fertilization experiment. They must conceive a
human larva for the good of the species. In the future,
it will be possible to obtain this precious larva through
an incubator, and a more sophisticated beaker, without
their presence, without their undressed bodies, without
the exhilarated clenching. Without tenderness. Without
their unnamed longing. Without desperation. This vision
has nothing to do with me. It leaves me cold. No, it is not
this either.

Now the hall is high and empty. The hall is in a temple or cathedral, a vast space, dark enough. In the middle of the hall there is a long table covered with a heavy,
red material. On top of it lies a woman. She wears a long,
white dress, and she does not move. A kind of priest
appears from somewhere, in long, black, and odd vestments, and beside the woman, with his arms outstretched,
holding golden instruments, he executes a complicated
ritual. He leaves and is replaced in a bit by another man.
Or the same man, without the long, black vestments. He
stares at the woman a long time, then cries loudly. He

adjusts the flowers in her hair, the folds of her dress that have fallen over the edge of the table. Next, he tries to kiss her, to embrace her, he stands on the tips of his toes, he climbs onto the table, over the woman, he rubs her with his hands, with his feet. The woman does not move, she does not budge. Then the man, crying loudly, takes out a knife and sticks it deep into the woman. I yelp involuntarily. The woman makes no sound, bleeds no drop of blood. I feel my mind go dark.

The window is half open and glitters in the afternoon sun. In the interior courtyard there is no one, no face at the windows, no movement. You continue to sleep deeply, calmly, your back toward me. On the other side, the young woman and young man have stopped their act of love. They are staring at each other. They are staring ecstatically at each other, as though a golden electric circuit bridged their eyes. In a perfect silence, I stare too, ecstatically. Without desire, pure. I have exhausted all the images. I feel empty, purified.

In the next moment, I know. Now I know. All these things are us. Exactly the two of us. In the antiseptic room, in the narrow, white bed, you move onto me gently. We must complete, without mistakes, an essential act, from which hangs our fate, ours and the world's. It seems as though we are not alone, as though we are in a large laboratory with glass walls, or onstage in an old, outdoor amphitheater, as though we are acting out a bizarre, archaic ritual in a high hall, a temple or church, watched by a host of unseen people.

Together, we must find a portal out of the world. I hear a deep vibration around us, like a low musical note, against which a neutral voice seems to recite from a holy, dusty book: "Love is good, love is pure, love is salvation, it is the greatest wonder of the world, do not be afraid, do not be ashamed," it whispers. You caress me constantly and whisper fervently, you whisper ceaselessly: "I know a way out of the world. I know a way out of the world. This way. This way we can escape. Do you want to? Do you want to?"

I start to tremble. Something I do not understand in your words frightens me. I am terrified, my flesh hurts. In between kisses and caresses, I respond to you fearfully, "What velvety skin! What beautiful thighs, so powerful! How nice it is here, beside you, with you! Who cares about the outside, the beyond?" You touch me, you love me, you whisper ceaselessly, "Do you want to, to go beyond? Do you want to escape?"

Vibrating like a chord about to snap, I might faint, my mind goes dark, I might die. With the last of my strength, I whisper to you, "But Mamma has to watch over us, at least! Mamma has to watch over us!"

Calm, precise, overwhelming, you murmur with

your lips on my ear, "Relax, we are not alone." And through the half-open window beside our narrow, white bed, which slowly and ineluctably tilts into the void, a thin, blond young man enters, wearing a short, white tunic. He smiles and looks at us encouragingly.

And then he tosses us, like a piece of gold jewelry, into the universe.

MORE THAN ONE
TYPE OF PERCEPTION

Let me tell you a secret, darling. I know you'll respond sarcastically: *Another one?* But I can't help it, I can't keep it to myself. It's something that could happen to you, that has to do with you, it's too important to keep quiet.

Did you know our sense organs perceive in more than one way? Something like the segments of a telescope that slide into each other, that sometimes snap together unexpectedly. *How do you know?* you ask. As I've told you before, darling, from experience. I don't theorize, I live. I don't repeat what others have said, and I don't quietly copy techniques and rituals down, I try to experiment. My science is epidermal, my knowledge is sensory. My metaphysics is strictly corporeal and psychic, my revelations come from the cellular abyss. I don't want just to know, I want to be that which I know. Or to be within that which I know. To become that which I know I can become, and even more. I cannot be satisfied with this repetitive existence, with this world trapped within the walls of the mind. I know there is more, much more.

But let me tell you the story.

•

First, there is everyday, banal perception, our common perception, imprecise and inattentive. For example, I walk down an unpaved country road, I see the pebbles on the ground, stuck in the yellow earth, but my mind moves quickly in another direction, I think about how much the train costs from Bucharest to Sinaia. I know that the gray rocks are there, in their irregular shapes, I kick some by accident, but now I am thinking of an article I read yesterday in an art magazine. In fact, the stones do not interest me, they are there, they must be there, low, under my shoes, this is enough, it's all the same. I am thinking now about the Retezat Mountains and what I'm going to eat this evening.

Then there is a somewhat clearer perception, a limpidness. The country road rises toward hills dotted with pine trees. And at a certain moment, a double ray of light slants down from a cloud to touch a stone, one of the many small stones that crunch under my feet. In the impact of that ray of light, the stone attracts my attention, seems to shine a little, seems to gain a face. I stop. I finally pay attention, I pick the stone up, I look at it insistently. It has an irregular oval shape, it has innumerable pocks and striations. The pocks look like holes in a piece of old, dried-out meat. The striations are colored gray, pink, and purple, and between them I see a gold line. Perhaps a valuable rock, I think in passing. Perhaps there is a vein of gold in the area. I turn the stone over in my hand, I don't see any other glint. I lose interest, it's just a regular stone. I throw it back on the road; without the ray of light, the stone loses its transformation. But my mind runs far from here, from the present. I think of the rock museum on Kiseleff Boulevard in the capital, and of my biology professor from long ago, from high school.

Then there is emotional perception. I am still on a narrow and steep mountain path, but somewhere else and some other time, when you and I are climbing to a faraway, isolated cabin in the Retezat Mountains. You are ahead of me on the path, I can hear the knock of your walking stick, I see only the soles of your heavy boots, since I am always looking down so as not to trip on broken rocks on the path. I am not looking at you, but I feel your body, your presence, the smell of your sweaty T-shirt, the heat of your sun-warmed skin. You are ahead of me and close, your body attracts me, calms me, lets me believe in my own existence. And in a moment, I know *objectively* that I love your body. As though my attraction for your body could become palpable, almost concrete, as though the energy of this feeling would materialize without itself, as a kind of denser air we could sense. I see this dense air somehow without my eyes, I feel it outside my body, as a self-evident *given*, like a transparent object that I cannot avoid acknowledging, since it occupies a kind of noticeable space. Its invisible obviousness surprises me, I feel a warmth in my solar plexus that seems to wake me from sleep. And I have a moment of odd, intense lucidity.

Now I see everything around me with this emotional gaze. The outlines of all the shapes around me, the trees and cliffs, are precise and clear, but they are also strangely alive, vibrant. I look down again, at the path. I see the bits of crushed rock, I see them with an unusually concentrated attention. I cannot think of anything, I am full of this intense, expanded attention. And at that moment I realize that I love them, I love the bits of crushed rock. I am connected to them through an odd wave of energy.

Then I enter another perception. The rocks around me become more and more beautiful, more expressive, as though scales and translucid skins were falling from my eyes, and my retina were cleaned, and the crystal of my eyes had smoke cleared away, a veil or a fog removed. The shapes of the rocks *tell* me more and more, even though I cannot mentally formulate what exactly, they seem like mysterious and almost living presences, like three-dimensional hieroglyphs, given form in space, just about to show something, to reveal a mystery. I understand then that these rocks are precious stones. They are jewels of every color, they are jades, opals, agates, pearls, quartz crystals, and gold nuggets, they are emeralds, rubies, tige-reyes, and diamonds. This is their true essence. Brilliance. Light. But a brilliance also captive. A rainbow light suddenly and mysteriously solidified. Only my banal, dormant eyes saw them as muted, washed-out, ugly. Only my unloving and inattentive gaze gave them an opaque layer of ash. But they, these stone jewels, are patient. They wait. They are waiting just for this long, ecstatic *moment*. They have been waiting since the beginning of creation.

And then, with a little luck, in moments of grace, it is possible to enter a completely other perception. Although you see everything as clearly as possible, like a luminous summer day, now you no longer perceive differences. Differences between stones and animals, between butterflies and flowers, between birds and vegetation, between people and trees, between clouds and earth, although you can still distinguish all these things perfectly well. But they are all, or they all become, the same vivid presence, a kind of coagulated light, full of energy, in particular manifestations; growing out of the earth, flowing, running, beating its wings, breathing, all are the same enormous, living intelligence expressing itself in chirps, rustlings, and words. Everything is identical in its essence, it is, how to put it, vibrant, alive, I mean it is sacred, because it is full of an immense joy and deep fear. Everything amazes, everything is ecstatic, everything is holy, because a giant something seems to descend through all things, continuously coming into the world and expressing itself. Clouds are the psychic states of the planet. Rivers are the blood system of the terrestrial crust. Geography breathes, it undulates like the curved shapes of a giant woman, forests are the planet's hair. Sparrows wear a minuscule angelic mask on their beaks. Two white butterflies resting on a daisy unfold their wings into a transparent cross of Calvary. The entire world is intelligent, is sacred, is full of the divine, is God. Boundless joy is divine, is God. This perception is God.

Immense Love, do not abandon me, help my eyes to be reborn, wash away their dirt and cataracts, clean off their banality and fear, break the veil of resistance, of refusal! Beauty and goodness of the world, do not abandon me, help my weakness, my laziness, my forgetfulness, my sleep! Do not leave me, immense Love, help me see through eyes of flesh with other eyes, clairvoyant eyes, with another gaze, a penetrating, limitless gaze, with another thought, supersensory thought, divine! Help my awakened eye pass through flesh and earth and stone and wood and opaque material unto you! Help my awakened and finally *real* thought be one with you!

There is more than one kind of perception. Those of the future.

MANDALA

Let me pour you another vodka, darling, now that you've come back, now that you want to leave again, and this time for good. Listen, I know you can barely stand to listen to me, but let me tell you another story. As I told you at the start, I want to free myself from this pulsating inner enigma, from this radioactive store of images I've carried within me so long. Darling, don't think bad of me; now that there is nothing left to lose, I can admit the following things.

I have, from time to time, an odd dream I can't understand. I, as a woman, am making love in the position a man usually takes. I am on top, I embrace, I caress, I kiss, I enter someone rhythmically, some body, but I can't see who. It's dark, I'm bathed in a warm, deep silence, I'm in the middle of a wide and, how can I put it, a prehistoric bed, at the bottom of an old, archaic cavern. And there is no one else. I'm alone, it's like I'm making love to myself, I embrace myself, I penetrate myself, I love myself—or maybe I'm making love to the dark. The darkness is alive, palpable, I rub it, I form it, I smack it with a kind of tender spite. The tension rises, as does the excitement, the fury. I don't feel with my entire skin anymore, with its softness and its frissons of every type, as I do when I make love as a woman; the liquid magic I once felt is concentrated now into a single point, in the burning, mad tip of my masculine sex, it forgets everything else and wants to finish at any price, to discharge itself, to free itself.

And when I reach the climax, when I catch fire like a rocket and release all that burns within, when I explode and discharge this fast, unbearable energy, something unexpected happens: the cloud of melted coals stops at the base of my abdomen, it does not go out but turns inward and upward, through my body, through the organs, toward my head. I feel a small wave within, warm and disturbing, that retreats like a sheet of hot water from my arteries and veins, nerves and tissues, and wants to climb higher and higher, up to my brain. And the moment it reaches my head, in the middle of my cranium, there is a sudden luminous explosion, a blinding discharge, and I wake up! I'm in my bed, it's night, I am flooded with a powerful joy. I do not know who I am, I am only a boundless consciousness that fills the darkness around me, I am the whole darkness, warm, living, conscious, that is one with the universe, also warm, also living, also conscious.

Then sometimes I dream about a pregnant man. Darling, he is a good-looking, well-made man, a bit like you, but with particular eyes: tender, emotional, with a golden, playful glint. His long, wavy hair hangs down to the small of his back. He walks about the room, his odd knot hanging flaccid and childish between his thighs. I look at his swollen abdomen, he has a stomach round as an enormous ball, with stretched and shining skin. From time to time, the man rubs his abdomen in pleasure, and he holds it from below with his large, powerful hands gingerly, carefully. His body has a bizarre but complete beauty. I caress his stomach slowly, I feel tender, delicate kicks inside. I feel a perfect satisfaction, a deep joy, as though I were the cause of that wonder. The man for his part also seems happy with what is happening to him, like a fruit that has finally produced seeds, like a galactic spiral that has finally located its mysterious center. Exhilarated like a pagan god in his fulfilled body, charmed by himself as any other pregnant creature would be, anyone who carries a new being inside, a new world, a new universe. Now he knows. He will give birth to a better humanity, one more beautiful, gentler. He will start by giving birth to a daughter.

Darling, tell me what would happen if a young man who lamented his own existence decided, as a result of this hysterical, exasperatingly fragmented world, this extroverted and forgetful world, to try an experiment in the service of humanity, to go beyond himself, to become a kind of Christ? And if a young woman, lamenting herself and the world in which she is given to live, a world blinded by cynicism and indifference, hermetically enclosed in its inexpungible carcasses, a world where it seems either no one can or no one wants to save anything, decided to give herself up, to become a kind of Christ? What would they need, each of them, or both of them together, to understand and to do? To provoke a new exterior revolution, or revelation? To invent a new way of doing things or a weapon of mass hypnosis—or to produce a kind of soft, interior dynamite in the brain to blow it up in strong images and to make it feel immense, to see without limits, to understand reality as it is, in all its levels, all its infra- and supersensory resonances: the total, essential reality? Like a veil removed from the eyes. Like a gentle, offhand enlightenment. Like a sudden opening of the sky in the middle of the head. Like a new, superemotional energy.

•

Darling, a little while ago, walking past a white house in the residential section of our provincial city, the one you want to leave, my gaze fell upon something so fascinating I had to stop. In the front yard, on well-tended, short-mown grass, there was a large, round basket woven from beautiful yellow-gold vines. Inside were about a dozen cats, all perfectly white, without a spot on their fur. Big cats and kittens, jumbled together in lascivious and silly poses, big cats licking each other and licking the kittens. Their owner, an older man, stood beside the basket and stared at them, in ecstasy. He told me proudly that they were all one family. That they were only females. The oldest cat was the great-great-grandmother of the others, her daughters, granddaughters, and great-granddaughters. They lay all around each other in this round woven basket, they cared for each other, groomed each other, played, teased, and loved each other, the great-grandmother and grandmothers and mothers cleaned the newborn kittens and fed them from their small pink nipples, all in calm, complete harmony. A white and spherical world that seemed to constantly give birth to itself, it lived within its own creation and returned identical to itself.

A total world, sufficient unto itself, that gave birth to itself in eternity and did not suffer degradation and death.

This image remained embossed in my mind, it marked me somehow, there was something just and calming in it that reconciled me to myself, to you, to the world. After I walked on, I replayed the memory many times, the golden basket with white cats, like a circular, living picture, like a pulsating mandala. The golden circle, the pattern of undulating curves ceaselessly recreated by the white, moving felines, the image filled my interior space, it projected itself onto the dome of my brain with a pure, enigmatic joy.

This surprising mandala, found in a woven basket, stayed with me for days and days; I put it into my collection of *powerful images*. You think it is just fashionable feminism, which, of course, you detest in your soul, as a man, even as you make an effort to appear understanding and tolerant on the outside. You're wrong, it's more complicated, deeper perhaps, more atavistic, with no connection to the world without. There is something in this image, a magic that makes me vibrate within, an emotional key that enters an unsoundable nucleus, hidden somewhere, in the abyss within the chest. From something that wants to erupt, to get out, but cannot. Because the exit code is blocked.

Who blocked it? Why, for what purpose? I do not

know, no one knows anymore. Certain exterior images suddenly remind me of a different kingdom, a real kingdom even though it has no palpable substance, a *kingdom of essential images*. Found somewhere *on the other side* of reality, between the sky and earth, between within and without. In fact, within us is the strange place that coincides with the cosmic, through a profound superimposition, through a primal identity. I sometimes have the strange hunch, a powerful and nostalgic intuition, that at one time we all existed within this colorful, joyful kingdom, and we could live quite well in the world of grandiose visions, within ourselves, as commodious as the universe. Something happened, an error, a fall, an inversion, and many images flowed outside and solidified. They hardened, like lava, in the cold exterior gravity, forced to condense and to shatter into millions of mountains, cliffs, rocks, stones, and pebbles. And sand, a lot of sand. But sometimes, a rivulet of that first lava penetrates our gaze in all its initial, blinding intensity. It is as though a veil retreated for a few seconds from our darkened eyes and our blocked minds, and then splinters from the splendid and majestic spectacle of the primal universe can touch our brain. Like fluttering visions, like an interior aurora borealis. As broken and fragmentary as they are, as apparently aberrant and absurd, these eruptions remain vital. Without them we might completely lose our bearings, because we could not access the initial ecstasy without them, the initial joy and limitlessness, we would lack the energy to continue to live and to understand the world outside and to strive to surpass it, we would dry up like plants cut off from their old roots that reach into the cosmos. We would lose contact with the Source.

But only if, through an odd mutation, the dreaming plants we are would develop longer and longer rhizomes, extending farther and farther from their points of departure, and would learn to grow roots in the void and to feed on nothingness and abstraction and to colonize with these tentacles a bare and instrumentalized universe, to spread a new humanity, strictly functional, strictly rational. Without an emotional organ. Without a living, true imagination. Without an all-encompassing love.

Darling, I know you prefer television and the internet, there you have all you want and don't want, evening after evening you gulp down a cocktail of films, talk shows, and news programs, computer games and links, sites, and blogs of every color; it's your cheap drug, it's democratic and beloved, it kills your time and dazzles your brain's circumvolutions. But you are allowing yourself to be blinded by images from outside, from outside your being, from the global collective mind; you stop paying attention to your inner film, it spills out of you like a hidden river and it waits, it waits for you, while you let yourself drown in a sea of strange images, whatever they are, banal or aggressive, dirty or criminal, and so you deplete your visionary power. That which reconciles you to yourself, with your whole self, and makes you one with the universe. The beauty without is no equal to the beauty within you; vibrating, shining from the depths, it feeds you and balances you and, who knows, it might make you limitless. Darling, even you have rich images hidden there in your unknown abyss, they glitter like fragile, forgotten gems; in their condensed, bizarre way they point to something you have known for a long time, perhaps forever, something you just do not want to remember. Even you have a collection of precious visions, you've just forbidden yourself from admitting they are there. Darling, let your deep interior images invade you, feed on the intense milk of emotion and the hard water of living attention. Darling, live off the essential images until they begin to vibrate within you, to pulsate, to illuminate, and to open subtle channels in your brain that lead to the limitless sky. A bridge of vibration, an ethereal trampoline toward the other world.

A MOMENT OF PRESENCE

There I sat, on the rickety, green park bench. The luminous afternoon approached its end; I was thinking about myself for the millionth time, looking with wonder, and desire as well, at myself, at my young, surprising body, assembled from curves, planes, and bulges, my woman's body, both detested and adored, my amazing receptacle of states and images.

I was waiting for you. The beloved, the adored, the detested. Example of an especially aggressive, absurd species, wanting to lose yourself at any price, to destroy yourself, to escape your species for something, someone else, anything, for things, sex, ideas, people, the world, anything but the species itself. An incomplete, forgetful species.

I look around myself carefully. You are late, as always, even for this final meeting. This long, odd waiting, when everything seems suddenly suspended. I feel a small tug at my heart, followed by a kind of emptiness in my stomach. I feel suspended, too. There is a lot of silence in this park, as the light of sunset slowly steals over.

Late in the day, you make your appearance. Someone else has sat on the bench in the meantime, an older woman, small, dressed completely in white, with a smiling face that reminds me of something calming and familiar. It's okay, it's okay, let's go have a drink. Around here, nowhere too far, there must be a restaurant or bar near the lake.

There is no one, at this hour, in the restaurant on the island in the middle of the lake. The waiter greets us apathetically, distantly. We sit facing the water, on white metal chairs. The lake waters are deep green, turbulent, with dark flashes. A lake of melted, undulating glass. You order your usual, double vodka on ice. I order a Martini.

We sit at the table quietly, the alcohol evaporates slowly from our glasses. We stare lazily at the expanse of water that surrounds us, its green glints, its hypnotic flashes. Our silence hollows me out, it hurts. We are like two halves of a coin split down the middle, symmetrical and yet opposite, which cannot come back together, two shiny metal spheres attracting and repelling each other in equal force, instead of fusing, two parallel columns of light shining upward, searching for a common sky without ever finding it. We drink, we are quiet, I feel nothing but a small flash of pain in my cerebral hemispheres, encompassed by silence, then by pressure, as though something heavy and viscous wanted to descend and to be understood. I look at you, I let myself feel a warm, odd tension that makes me vibrate slightly. I attend without thought to my own presence in this mute and almost unmoving scene, whose contours are becoming more evident, I attend to something strange, a silent film that runs separate from me, on a studio set, in a beautifully colorful scene. I am here, present to myself, present to you. And somehow detached.

We are actors in this film, a banal, ridiculous melodrama, but this enormous quantity of feelings must have a meaning, even as they are consumed pointlessly, in a crowd of mismatching incongruities. I sit beside you, I want to send a silent emotion, a state, but you start talking to me. I know that you're saying something clear and final, explaining rationally, logically, point by point, why there can be nothing between us, and yet I do not completely understand what you're saying, I cannot listen to your precise words with complete attention. I feel nothing more than the fact that we are living through this bittersweet moment, whose melancholic denouement will never be repeated. I do not want to understand, I just want to feel, to record it somewhere apart from myself, because my mind forgets too quickly. To feel how a rarefied air unites me to you, how an aerial water moves from me toward you and toward the emerald-green water around the restaurant. How my awakened consciousness, concentrated in my heart, makes me and all the shapes around us vibrate, it dissolves me gently into the leaves and people at the other tables. Something in my body, a hidden place behind my sternum, understands this scene better than my mind does, with another kind of intelligence.

I know we must leave each other, a time must pass, I must remember this day, this hour, this final meeting, must repeat it to myself in all its details, the restaurant, the table, and the white metal chairs, the glasses of vodka and the Martini, in order to feel suddenly, in a flash, the extraordinary in this moment, that moment, which I am already living from the future to the past, as though it were a vibrant-painful image from the middle of my chest. The depth of my presence in the film of this moment. Of *presence*.

We sit at the table, we are silent, the alcohol evaporates slowly from our glasses. We gaze listlessly toward our surroundings. Water, shadow, rustling leaves in the declining light. Undulating surfaces, towers of leaves, where I see what could be women in profile, young women, tall and proud women, beautiful women who remind me of a terrible beauty, passing on the path, in the distance. We sip from our glasses. The mental desert, an unknown spot before our eyes, expanses of lapping waters, distance. We drink. I am extremely close and extremely far from you. Something within me still wants to coincide with you. Silently, something sends you a scream.

A sphere of lightning appears before my inner vision, like an enormous, soft eyeball removed from its socket. Its golden sphere looks directly into me, behind the lid, it penetrates. What does it want to say, why did it appear, what does it remind me of? A danger vibrates again around me, an imminence.

Then I no longer see anything within me but fields of blue, great expanses of calm, bare water, undulating life, life like a mist over the waters under low, transparent skies, great solitary expanses of water, water everywhere, only water, sea everywhere, only the sea, I see an ocean everywhere, nothing but undulating, azure blue, and then suddenly, somewhere in the middle of the expanse, a fountain, a kind of vertical water and light, a rainbow as straight as an arrow, it is a vertical path in seven colors that climbs toward the sky, red-orange-yellow-green-blue-in-digo-violet, it widens to cover the whole sky, oh, its edges are grass and summer flowers, what fresh banks, dear mother!, what an ocean of light, what deep, blue calm! Let's climb it, darling, climb up this vertical path, let's climb! It is an elevator to *the other world.*

We sit at a table, we drink a Martini and a vodka, the alcohol evaporates slowly from the glasses of our beings. I see a small turtle carefully crossing the restaurant patio. It will cross like this, carefully, for eternity. We look at the world around us, this world that constantly forgets, as you and I forget; the sphere of lightning pointlessly crosses our gaze. What does it want, there above, in the emotional sky, what does it foretell? I look more carefully at you, the detested, the beloved. Your gaze is muddy, a sign that the alcohol has done its job, you stare at the lake, the flashing green, undulating green, vibrant green, green, green, you look at it almost hypnotized, a kind of light blossoms over your face, I think you've begun to see, *to see* in a way you've contracted from me, from my vibrations, then you laugh quietly, as though you were suffering and enjoying yourself at the same time, laughing and crying, going crazy and finally becoming sane. In the end, through your teeth, you spit out a delectable expletive.

THE GREAT CHESS GAME

Darling, they say that men and women are improvising actors,
pushed onto the stage for an hour under the powerful lights. In
fact, as I have said, they are in a complicated game of chess,
on the great board of the world, with different-colored squares
under different lights. I know, darling, that others have discov-
ered the same thing, but I've only recently learned this amaz-
ing fact. We are living chess pieces, and, at the same time,
we are the chess players. Almost every daily act, a gesture
desired and missed, an apparently happenstance meeting,
every momentary choice between paying attention to yourself
and falling asleep, every spell of laziness in the middle of con-
centration, every moment of forgetting, every time we hurry
for no reason to end a hug, every small and apparently benign
moment of forgetfulness, everything minuscule and grand
changes the complicated stage on which we live, and, because
of the dimensions of the game, we cannot see the results of
our moves. The black and white squares, or whatever color
they are, are sometimes enormous, other times tiny, around

*them are mountain peaks and ravines with dirty water; per-
spective changes at a dizzying speed, to the side, in a circle, in
a spiral, up or down. Sometimes, the chess pieces have forms
we know from home, they are those dear to us, lovers, friends,
and family, other times they are strange apparitions, visions
in the middle of the day, dreams and premonitions, surprising coincidences. Sometimes the moves are made outside of
us, other times within, other times within and without, but
the rules of the game seem to constantly change, as I've told
you, but the game, in all its mysterious, dancing beauty, is not
damaged or changed.*

*In fact, the rules don't change, but our points of refer-
ence do, as well as our contradicting expectations. Because
what the game asks you to do is to pay more and more attention as it goes on, to be more present and more fluid. To read
between the signs and happenings, the visions and unexpected significations. To allow a more ample thought to bloom
with all its petals within you. To understand that in spite of
the appearance of chaos and the complicated, senseless charades, there are still natural laws in this life, emotional, spir-
itual, and cosmic laws that you may count on. You are the
piece and you are the player. Your being is your tool and your
path. On the other side of the immense chessboard is your
more ample counterpart, a corresponding projection, a vast
and invisible player—in fact multiple players, energies and
natural laws, vital psychic forces, levels of your depths and*

of your supermind—or let's say, like we used to, demons and gods, cosmic explorers and guardian angels, transparent and impersonal tutors, with a vast and nuanced intelligence, on whose equanimity and patience one may, in the end, rely. They often send you signs, dreams, and visions in their enigmatic language, but how concrete it is, how all-encompassing. You might, if you have the courage to decipher the self-enclosed games, try to make a draw with a universe that seems to have no exit, or perhaps even a little checkmate with death.

Darling, there is a higher order in all the chaos of our lives, one that has a subtle objectivity and is therefore hard to perceive, but one we can count on. It presents itself to us only rarely, as a burst of impressions of limitlessness, like the scent of a strange and ineffable understanding, that stupefies our senses and exhilarates our cerebral meanderings. This vast and invisible order, when you glimpse it, comes like an awakening, like a revelation, like a form of amazing joy, immense happiness and reconciliation. We all have access to it from time to time, when we fall in love or in flashes of detached and visionary lucidity, when we are present to the pure and full and amazing reality of this world, that is to say, in moments of grace.

On one condition: that we do not forget that it's all, in the end, a dance, a play, a game. The great game we play with ourselves and the world, with which we in fact become one. A mythical game that includes the seas and mountains and forests and living creatures of every type, it includes the geology of the planet and the psychic abyss and interstellar space. A game of chess with the whole universe, which, pure and simple, plays with us. A game with the other side.

THE LITTLE ONE

That's when I saw you, child. Finally, you came! Yet you were odd. I did not expect you to be like this. Like a luminous point in a corner of the ceiling, like a spark of flying fire. From there, from above, you stared at me, in hope and fear. You were very small, a luminous and uneasy smidge of something that wanted to descend into the world, to become incarnate, to grow. A vague and gentle vibration wafted intermittently from you. You wanted to know if I wanted you, if I desired you.

I felt you constantly there, over my room. And in the end, I had the courage to open myself, to receive you, to let you take root. In my basket of bones and flesh, in the minuscule sarcophagus behind my sternum. You were there, a minuscule, white child, floating on dark and warm waters, over which the dawn broke timidly. Then you began to rise and grow. At first you were as big as a bean, round and white. Then you were as big as a walnut, or a chestnut. You grew as large as a lemon, as an orange, leaping across the waves of an unseen sea, along the fluttering eyelash of light, growing ever more quickly.

Then I began to see your details more clearly. The delicate hands and feet. Like fish fins, or a lizard's soft feet. The happy and luminous little face, with intense, penetrating eyes, yellow hair with short, thin curls fluttering around your head like a tiny halo, all of it wrapped my chest in sweetness. The pinkish disk of your face appeared on the horizon.

Then you became as large as a pumpkin. Your body was still transparent and delicate. Your eyes began to blink. Quickly, dizzyingly, you rose, you grew, you were already larger than me, even though you still had an infant's body. I saw your domed, shining cranium, your rose-colored cheeks with rounded cheekbones, the fine folds of skin under your chin, your wrists and knees, casting pink shadows over violet clouds from the horizon. Within my chest, it was morning.

You did not stop, you grew more. Round infant, giant silk cocoon, you grew higher than the trees on the street. The apartment blocks only came up to your armpits, your smile turned the far-off mountains gold and the top of your soft belly began to touch the clouds. You crossed the planet's atmosphere, with its air full of vague faces of men and women, transparent faces of people who once were, hazy faces of people who will be, myriads and myriads of faces that fill space, that shape the molecules and atoms of the volatile material of the air, using the vibrations of their past and future lives. I was already raised to the horizon.

And then higher, farther, you spread like a milky sea to the other planets, you sent your joyful laugh, like a sparkling cloud, to the other astral conglomerations. You were vast, little child, you filled space with your diffuse, sweet light, a light that jetted out from my chest, from under my sternum. You were immense and round, you laughed, you tumbled through the void. And I knew that this universe was still a child, it was alive and loved and wanted to be loved.

When you finally turned around to look at me, from the distance, I felt your unreal smile unfolding like a flaming rose with innumerable petals over my face, I could barely withstand its heat and brilliance. And yet I opened my eyes again and looked around. And what I saw amazed me.

Raised to the dome of the sky, at the zenith, I knew I was the World. In a deep and inexplicable way, I was one with all and with everything. I reached the sky and extended to the depths of the earth. I embraced all the earth from above as it unfolded. I felt the geological strata, the vegetation, the animals. I thought by means of the planets and their satellites and their interstellar trajectories. I

was, somewhere between high and low, a torrential, luminous, and loving consciousness. Suspended in an eternal
moment, I was illuminating and free, I was the Sun.

Then everything was snuffed out. I am back again in my
banal room in my apartment. A spark dances in front of
my eyes, perhaps it is just my weariness, or a firefly. I look
in the mirror, I see that my pupils are dilated, through
them I think I see a small, luminous figure. I flatten my
dress over my breasts, my hips. I caress my own abdomen. Who is inside whom? Who encompasses whom in
this mysterious world? And who thinks of whom, in the
end; who thinks through whom, in this story? The image
of the child returns to my mind, a light comes forth, a
deep, odd joy. I ask myself where this desperate hope
comes from. Absurd questions buzz in my mind, which
has become again limited, banal. I have a hard day tomorrow, full of things to do, tomorrow will be like today,
without you, alone, alone. Ah, but what is happening? I
don't feel well. I feel nauseous. Why does my chest hurt?
What is kicking in my stomach?

REVELATION

Darling, we have come to the end. Your neighborhood Scheherazade, who has irritated you and worn you out, is finished with her stories and charades for a while. Make no mistake, I have never taken drugs. I do not know how cocaine tastes, or opium, I've never tried LSD or mescaline. Where I come from, these things were not available, they weren't easy to find, I only read about drugs in books. The drug I use is completely personal, it is within. I give it to myself alone, meditating, praying, looking at the sunset and sunrise, reading certain poems or books that lift me to special mental spheres or stimulate my unconscious, but more often than not, I don't unleash this effect, rather it comes from a mysterious contact with the other side. My narcotic is found only in the brain, in the sweet endorphins that bathe my neurons, as numerous as the dust of the cosmos, but endorphins are nothing but a chemical trace through my hemispheric circumvolutions, suddenly tuned to I do not know what knowledge of wholeness. My brain becomes an expanded organ, receptive to the visions that exist, preexist *probably, in another world, in a world of invisible resonances, found everywhere and nowhere, in a field of forces we still know too little of, where a memory is kept, larger, older, and more archaic.*

Darling, these visions come from their own kingdom, from other worlds, from within and without, from a kingdom that exists in a dimension that as yet escapes us. These visions are not as strictly individual as they seem, they do not belong to me completely, they only pass through me as though I were an electric cable, a satellite antenna, they just borrow a little incarnation from me, that is why I must tell you their stories, must bear witness. They belong to a more encompassing intelligence, something vaster, one that includes us and wants nothing more than to manifest itself through us, so that we can see it. To see Reality. So we may be Reality. That reality that hasn't been degraded by our primitive and fearful senses, or by our deeply terrified mental programming. Reality as it is in itself, wondrous, infinite. A perfectly coherent reality, deeply loving. Its flash of perception equals revelation. It is, actually, Revelation.

Darling, I needed to liberate my brain from these visions, to leave them behind, solidified. To leave them like the shells of odd, exotic snails, on the impersonal beach of a memory detached from myself. To leave them behind like testimonies, like concrete proofs, on the yellow sand, fine and damp, on the shores of this deep world, this giant aquarium full of turbulent water, from which somehow, I do not know how, I might escape, might extract myself for a moment. I could toss myself onto the shore, onto the other side, to suffocate myself in the new air, in the too-pure ether, to feel like I might lose consciousness. To believe I have died. And then to find, I do not know how, that I escaped this shell for a moment, that I can rise, I can breathe again, I can fly. With another understanding, with another state of being.

Darling, I needed to discharge these odd visions. To put them into your brain, because you need this food, even if you still won't accept it. To put them there like minuscule eggs of a species of coleoptera on the path to extinction, one that wants to know how to burst into the world. How to achieve revelation. That is, Reality.

Darling, I have been reached by only a trifling number of the visions that are suspended, vibrating, in their vast, under-explored kingdom, only those that have been willing to descend along my emotional wavelength, but the rest of them are waiting for us. Darling, try to provoke contact with this mysterious intelligence hidden in the depths and heights of your body. If I can, you can too, now that you know it is possible. Now that you know this is the way to Reality.

1995–2005. 2010

Thank you all
for your support.
We do this for you,
and could not do
it without you.

PARTNERS

AVAILABLE NOW FROM DEEP VELLUM

AMANG · *Raised by Wolves*
translated by Steve Bradbury · TAIWAN

MICHÈLE AUDIN · *One Hundred Twenty-One Days*
translated by Christiana Hills · FRANCE

BAE SUAH · *Recitation*
translated by Deborah Smith · SOUTH KOREA

EDUARDO BERTI · *The Imagined Land*
translated by Charlotte Coombe · ARGENTINA

CARMEN BOULLOSA · *Texas: The Great Theft* · *Before* · *Heavens on Earth*
translated by Samantha Schnee · Peter Bush · Shelby Vincent · MEXICO

LEILA S. CHUDORI · *Home*
translated by John H. McGlynn · INDONESIA

SARAH CLEAVE, ed. · *Banthology: Stories from Banned Nations* ·
IRAN, IRAQ, LIBYA, SOMALIA, SUDAN, SYRIA & YEMEN

ANANDA DEVI · *Eve Out of Her Ruins*
translated by Jeffrey Zuckerman · MAURITIUS

ALISA GANIEVA · *Bride and Groom* · *The Mountain and the Wall*
translated by Carol Apollonio · RUSSIA

ANNE GARRÉTA · *Sphinx* · *Not One Day*
translated by Emma Ramadan · FRANCE

JÓN GNARR · *The Indian* · *The Pirate* · *The Outlaw*
translated by Lytton Smith · ICELAND

GOETHE · *The Golden Goblet: Selected Poems*
translated by Zsuzsanna Ozsváth and Frederick Turner · GERMANY

NOEMI JAFFE · *What Are the Blind Men Dreaming?*
translated by Julia Sanches & Ellen Elias-Bursac · BRAZIL

CLAUDIA SALAZAR JIMÉNEZ · *Blood of the Dawn*
translated by Elizabeth Bryer · PERU

PERGENTINO JOSÉ · *Red Ants: Stories*
translated by Tom Bunstead and the author · MEXICO

JUNG YOUNG MOON · *Seven Samurai Swept Away in a River* · *Vaseline Buddha*
translated by Yewon Jung · SOUTH KOREA

FOWZIA KARIMI · *Above Us the Milky Way: An Illuminated Alphabet* · USA

KIM YIDEUM · *Blood Sisters*
translated by Ji yoon Lee · SOUTH KOREA

TAISIA KITAISKAIA · *The Nightgown & Other Poems* · USA

JOSEFINE KLOUGART · *Of Darkness*
translated by Martin Aitken · DENMARK

YANICK LAHENS · *Moonbath*
translated by Emily Gogolak · HAITI

FOUAD LAROUI · *The Curious Case of Dassoukine's Trousers*
translated by Emma Ramadan · MOROCCO

DMITRY LIPSKEROV · *The Tool and the Butterflies*
translated by Reilly Costigan-Humes & Isaac Stackhouse Wheeler · RUSSIA

FORTHCOMING FROM DEEP VELLUM

MARIO BELLATIN · *Mrs. Murakami's Garden*
translated by Heather Cleary · MEXICO

MAGDA CARNECI · *FEM*
translated by Sean Cotter · ROMANIA

MIRCEA CĂRTĂRESCU · *Solenoid*
translated by Sean Cotter · ROMANIA

MATHILDE CLARK · *Lone Star*
translated by Martin Aitken · DENMARK

LOGEN CURE · *Welcome to Midland: Poems* · USA

PETER DIMOCK · *Daybook from Sheep Meadow* · USA

CLAUDIA ULLOA DONOSO · *Little Bird*, translated by Lily Meyer · PERU/NORWAY

LEYLÂ ERBIL · *A Strange Woman*
translated by Nermin Menemencioğlu · TURKEY

ROSS FARRAR · *Ross Sings Cheree & the Animated Dark: Poems* · USA

FERNANDA GARCIA LAU · *Out of the Cage*
translated by Will Vanderhyden · ARGENTINA

ANNE GARRÉTA · *In/concrete*
translated by Emma Ramadan · FRANCE

GOETHE · *Faust, Part One*
translated by Zsuzsanna Ozsváth and Frederick Turner · GERMANY

JUNG YOUNG MOON · *Arriving in a Thick Fog*
translated by Mah Eunji and Jeffrey Karvonen · SOUTH KOREA

FISTON MWANZA MUJILA · *The Villain's Dance*, translated by Roland
Glasser · *The River in the Belly: Selected Poems*, translated by Bret Maney ·
DEMOCRATIC REPUBLIC OF CONGO

LUDMILLA PETRUSHEVSKAYA · *Kidnapped: A Crime Story*, translated by
Marian Schwartz ·
The New Adventures of Helen: Magical Tales, translated by Jane Bugaeva ·
RUSSIA

JULIE POOLE · *Bright Specimen: Poems from the Texas Herbarium* · USA

MANON STEFAN ROS · *The Blue Book of Nebo* · WALES

ETHAN RUTHERFORD · *Farthest South & Other Stories* · USA

BOB TRAMMELL · *The Origins of the Avant-Garde in Dallas & Other Stories* · USA